P9-CFC-739

Leaving Home

Leaving Home

Stories selected by
Hazel Rochman
& Darlene Z. McCampbell

HarperCollins*Publishers*

Leaving Home: *Stories*
Copyright © 1997 by Hazel Rochman and Darlene Z. McCampbell
Page 232 represents an extension of the copyright page. All rights reserved. No part of this book may be used or reproduced in any manner whatsoever without written permission except in the case of brief quotations embodied in critical articles and reviews. Printed in the United States of America. For information address HarperCollins Publishers, 10 East 53rd Street, New York, NY 10022. http://www.harpercollins.com

Library of Congress Cataloging-in-Publication Data
  Leaving home : stories / selected by Hazel Rochman and Darlene Z. McCampbell.
     p.   cm.
  Summary: An international anthology that reflects the thoughts and feelings of young people as they make their own ways into the world.
     ISBN 0-06-024873-4. — ISBN 0-06-024874-2 (lib. bdg.) —
  ISBN 0-06-440706-3 (pbk.)
     1. Youth—Juvenile fiction.   2. Short stories.   [1. Short stories.]   I. Rochman, Hazel.
II. McCampbell, Darlene Z.
PZ5.L55   1997   96-28979
[Fic]—dc20   CIP
                                                                             AC

Typography by Al Cetta and Michele N. Tupper   ❖   First paperback edition, 1998

Contents

Whoever you are: some evening take a step
out of your house, which you know so well.
Enormous space is near . . .

RILKE

Introduction

There are times when everyone feels stuck at home. Shut in. It seems that everything is happening somewhere else. Or, you may feel stuck outside—on the margin— with your face pressed against the pane.

Nevertheless, everyone eventually goes on a journey. You leave home and undergo trials and rites; you come back from the journey transformed.

People have always told stories about these perilous journeys. The journey may be to war. It may be on a boat across the ocean to the United States from Europe, or from Southeast Asia. It may be on a bus in the night. But the journey can also be close to home—the turning of a corner to discover a whole new view of what was taken for granted, a discovery about someone you thought you knew, or a journey through the tangle of feelings in the human heart. It may happen on the day you start school, or the moment when you see your mother as a person separate from yourself.

You may make the journey alone—or you may go with a friend or a guide. The stories you read can transform you. They can help you imagine beyond yourself. When you read a great story you leave home.

We leave home to find home.

A House
of My Own

Sandra Cisneros

Not a flat. Not an apartment in back. Not a man's house. Not a daddy's. A house all my own. With my porch and my pillow, my pretty purple petunias. My books and my stories. My two shoes waiting beside the bed. Nobody to shake a stick at. Nobody's garbage to pick up after.

Only a house quiet as snow, a space for myself to go, clean as paper before the poem.

Saturday at the Canal

Gary Soto

I was hoping to be happy by seventeen.
School was a sharp check mark in the roll book,
An obnoxious tuba playing at noon because our team
Was going to win at night. The teachers were
Too close to dying to understand. The hallways
Stank of poor grades and unwashed hair. Thus,
A friend and I sat watching the water on Saturday,
Neither of us talking much, just warming ourselves
By hurling large rocks at the dusty ground
And feeling awful because San Francisco was a postcard
On a bedroom wall. We wanted to go there,
Hitchhike under the last migrating birds
And be with people who knew more than three chords
On a guitar. We didn't drink or smoke,
But our hair was shoulder length, wild when
The wind picked up and the shadows of
This loneliness gripped loose dirt. By bus or car,
By the sway of train over a long bridge,
We wanted to get out. The years froze
As we sat on the bank. Our eyes followed the water,
White-tipped but dark underneath, racing out of town.

The
First Day

Edward P. Jones

On an otherwise unremarkable September morning, long before I learned to be ashamed of my mother, she takes my hand and we set off down New Jersey Avenue to begin my very first day of school. I am wearing a checkered-like blue-and-green cotton dress, and scattered about these colors are bits of yellow and white and brown. My mother has uncharacteristically spent nearly an hour on my hair that morning, plaiting and replaiting so that now my scalp tingles. Whenever I turn my head quickly, my nose fills with the faint smell of Dixie Peach hair grease. The smell is somehow a soothing one now and I will reach for it time and time again before the morning ends. All the plaits, each with a blue barrette near the tip and each twisted into an uncommon sturdiness, will last until I go to bed that night, something that has never happened before. My stomach is full of milk and oatmeal sweetened with brown sugar. Like everything else I have on, my pale green slip and underwear are new, the underwear having come three to a plastic package with a little girl on the front who appears to be dancing. Behind my ears, my mother, to stop my whining, has dabbed the stingiest bit of her gardenia perfume, the last present my father gave her before he disappeared into memory. Because I cannot smell it, I have only her word that the perfume is there. I am also wearing yellow socks trimmed with thin lines of black and white around the tops. My shoes are my greatest joy, black patent-leather miracles, and when one is nicked at the toe later that morning in class, my heart will break.

I am carrying a pencil, a pencil sharpener, and a small ten-cent tablet with a black-and-white speckled cover. My mother does not believe that a girl in kindergarten needs such things, so I am taking them only because of my insistent whining and because they are presented from our neighbors, Mary Keith and Blondelle Harris. Miss Mary and Miss Blondelle are watching my two younger sisters until my mother returns. The women are as precious to me as my mother and sisters. Out playing one day, I have overheard an older child, speaking to another child, call Miss Mary and Miss Blondelle a word that is brand new to me. This is my mother: When I say the word in fun to one of my sisters, my mother slaps me across the mouth and the word is lost for years and years.

All the way down New Jersey Avenue, the sidewalks are teeming with children. In my neighborhood, I have many friends, but I see none of them as my mother and I walk. We cross New York Avenue, we cross Pierce Street, and we cross L and K, and still I see no one who knows my name. At I Street, between New Jersey Avenue and Third Street, we enter Seaton Elementary School, a timeworn, sad-faced building across the street from my mother's church, Mt. Carmel Baptist.

Just inside the front door, women out of the advertisements in *Ebony* are greeting other parents and children.

The woman who greets us has pearls thick as jumbo marbles that come down almost to her navel, and she acts as if she had known me all my life, touching my shoulder, cupping her hand under my chin. She is enveloped in a perfume that I only know is not gardenia. When, in answer to her question, my mother tells her that we live at 1227 New Jersey Avenue, the woman first seems to be picturing in her head where we live. Then she shakes her head and says that we are at the wrong school, that we should be at Walker-Jones.

My mother shakes her head vigorously. "I want her to go here," my mother says. "If I'da wanted her someplace else, I'da took her there." The woman continues to act as if she has known me all my life, but she tells my mother that we live beyond the area that Seaton serves. My mother is not convinced and for several more minutes she questions the woman about why I cannot attend Seaton. For as many Sundays as I can remember, perhaps even Sundays when I was in her womb, my mother has pointed across I Street to Seaton as we come and go to Mt. Carmel. "You gonna go there and learn about the whole world." But one of the guardians of that place is saying no, and no again. I am learning this about my mother: The higher up on the scale of respectability a person is—and teachers are rather high up in her eyes—the less she is liable to let them push her around. But finally, I see in her eyes the closing gate, and she takes my hand and we leave the building. On the steps, she stops as people move past us on either side.

"Mama, I can't go to school?"

She says nothing at first, then takes my hand again and

13

we are down the steps quickly and nearing New Jersey Avenue before I can blink. This is my mother: She says, "One monkey don't stop no show."

Walker-Jones is a larger, new school and I immediately like it because of that. But it is not across the street from my mother's church, her rock, one of her connections to God, and I sense her doubts as she absently rubs her thumb over the back of her hand. We find our way to the crowded auditorium where gray metal chairs are set up in the middle of the room. Along the wall to the left are tables and other chairs. Every chair seems occupied by a child or adult. Somewhere in the room a child is crying, a cry that rises above the buzz-talk of so many people. Strewn about the floor are dozens and dozens of pieces of white paper, and people are walking over them without any thought of picking them up. And seeing this lack of concern, I am all of a sudden afraid.

"Is this where they register for school?" my mother asks a woman at one of the tables.

The woman looks up slowly as if she has heard this question once too often. She nods. She is tiny, almost as small as the girl standing beside her. The woman's hair is set in a mass of curlers and all of those curlers are made of paper money, here a dollar bill, there a five-dollar bill. The girl's hair is arrayed in curls, but some of them are beginning to droop and this makes me happy. On the table beside the woman's pocketbook is a large notebook, worthy of someone in high school, and looking at me looking at the notebook, the girl places her hand possessively on it. In her other hand she holds several pencils with thick crowns of additional erasers.

"These the forms you gotta use?" my mother asks the

woman, picking up a few pieces of the paper from the table. "Is this what you have to fill out?"

The woman tells her yes, but that she need fill out only one.

"I see," my mother says, looking about the room. Then: "Would you help me with this form? That is, if you don't mind."

The woman asks my mother what she means.

"This form. Would you mind helpin' me fill it out?"

The woman still seems not to understand.

"I can't read it. I don't know how to read or write, and I'm askin' you to help me." My mother looks at me, then looks away. I know almost all of her looks, but this one is brand new to me. "Would you help me, then?"

The woman says "Why sure," and suddenly she appears happier, so much more satisfied with everything. She finishes the form for her daughter and my mother and I step aside to wait for her. We find two chairs nearby and sit. My mother is now diseased, according to the girl's eyes, and until the moment her mother takes her and the form to the front of the auditorium, the girl never stops looking at my mother. I stare back at her. "Don't stare," my mother says to me. "You know better than that."

Another woman out of the *Ebony* ads takes the woman's child away. Now, the woman says upon returning, let's see what we can do for you two.

My mother answers the questions the woman reads off the form. They start with my last name, and then on to the first and middle names. This is school, I think. This is going to school. My mother slowly enunciates each word of my name. This is my mother: As the questions go on, she takes from her pocketbook document after document, as if they will support my right to attend school, as if she has been saving them up for just this moment. Indeed, she takes out more papers than I have ever seen her do in other places: my birth certificate, my baptismal record, a doctor's letter concerning my bout with chicken pox, rent receipts, records of immunization, a letter about our public assistance payments, even her marriage license—every single paper that has anything even remotely to do with my five-year-old life. Few of the papers are needed here, but it does not matter and my mother continues to pull out the documents with the purposefulness of a magician pulling out a long string of scarves. She has learned that money is the beginning and end of everything in this world, and when the woman finishes, my mother offers her fifty cents, and the woman accepts it without hesitation. My mother and I are just about the last parent and child in the room.

My mother presents the form to a woman sitting in front of the stage, and the woman looks at it and writes something on a white card, which she gives to my mother. Before long, the woman who has taken the girl with the drooping curls appears from behind us, speaks to the sitting woman, and introduces herself to my mother and me. She's to be my teacher, she tells my mother. My mother stares.

We go into the hall, where my mother kneels down to me. Her lips are quivering. "I'll be back to pick you up at twelve o'clock. I don't want you to go nowhere. You just wait right here. And listen to every word she say." I touch her lips and press them together. It is an old, old game between us. She puts my hand down at my side, which is not part of the game. She stands and looks a

second at the teacher, then she turns and walks away. I
see where she has darned one of her socks the night
before. Her shoes make loud sounds in the hall. She
passes through the doors and I can still hear the loud
sounds of her shoes. And even when the teacher turns
me toward the classrooms and I hear what must be the
singing and talking of all the children in the world, I can
still hear my mother's footsteps above it all.

Dancer

Vickie Sears

T ell you just how it was with her. Took her to a dance not long after she come to live with us. Smartest thing I ever done. Seems like some old Eaglespirit woman saw her living down here and came back just to be with Clarissa.

Five years old she was when she come to us. Some foster kids come with lots of stuff, but she came with everything she had in a paper bag. Some dresses that was too short. A pair of pants barely holding a crotch. A pile of ratty underwear and one new nightgown. Mine was her third foster home in as many months. The agency folks said she was *so-cio-path-ic*. I don't know nothing from that. She just seemed like she was all full up with anger and scaredness like lots of the kids who come to me. Only she was a real loner. Not trusting nobody. But she ran just like any other kid, was quiet when needed. Smiled at all the right times. If you could get her to smile, that is. Didn't talk much, though.

Had these ferocious dreams, too. Real screamer dreams they were. Shake the soul right out of you. She'd be screaming and crying with her little body wriggling on the bed, her hair all matted up on her woody-colored face. One time I got her to tell me what she was seeing, and she told me how she was being chased by a man with a long knife what he was going to kill her with and nobody could hear her calling out for help. She didn't talk too much about them, but they was all bad like that one. Seemed the most fierce dreams I ever remember anybody ever having outside of a vision seek. They said her tribe was Assiniboin, but they weren't for certain. What was for sure was that she was a fine dark-eyed girl just meant for someone to scoop up for loving.

Took her to her first dance in September, like I said, not long after she came. It wasn't like I thought it would be a good thing to do. It was just that we was all going. Me, my own kids, some nieces and nephews and the other children who was living with us. The powwow was just part of what we done all the time. Every month. More often in the summer. But this was the regular first Friday night of the school year. We'd all gather up and go to the school. I was thinking on leaving her home with a sitter cause she'd tried to kill one of the cats a couple of days before. We'd had us a big talk and she was grounded, but, well, it seemed like she ought to be with us.

Harold, that's my oldest boy, he and the other kids was mad with her, but he decided to show her around anyhow. At the school he went through the gym telling people, "This here's my sister, Clarissa." Wasn't no fuss or anything. She was just another one of the kids. When they was done meeting folks, he put her on one of the bleachers near the drum and went to join the men. He was in that place where his voice cracks but was real proud to be drumming. Held his hand up to his ear even, some of the time. Anyhow, Clarissa was sitting there, not all that interested in the dance or drum, when Molly Graybull come out in her button dress. Her arms was all stretched out, and she was slipping around, preening on them spindles of legs that get skinnier with every year. She was well into her seventies, and I might as well admit, Molly had won herself a fair share of dance contests. So it wasn't no surprise how a little girl could get so fixated on Molly. Clarissa watched her move around-around-around. Then all the rest of the dancers after Molly. She sure took in a good eyeful. Fancy dance. Owl dance. Circle dance. Even a hoop dancer was visiting that night. Everything weaving all slow, then fast. Around-around until that child couldn't see nothing else. Seemed like she was struck silent in the night, too. Never had no dreams at all. Well, not the hollering kind anyways.

Next day she was more quiet than usual only I could see she was looking at her picture book and tapping the old one-two, one-two. Tapping her toes on the rug with the inside of her head going around and around. As quiet as she could be, she was.

A few days went on before she asks me, "When's there gonna be another dance?"

I tell her in three weeks. She just smiles and goes on outside, waiting on the older kids to come home from school.

The very next day she asks if she can listen to some singing. I give her the tape recorder and some of Joe Washington from up to the Lummi reservation and the Kicking Woman Singers. Clarissa, she takes them tapes and runs out back behind the chicken shed, staying out all afternoon. I wasn't worried none, though, cause I could hear the music the whole time. Matter of fact, it like to make me sick of them same songs come the end of three weeks. But that kid, she didn't get into no kind of mischief.

Almost abnormal how good she was. Worried me some to see her so caught up but it seemed good too. The angry part of her slowed down so's she wasn't hitting the animals or chopping on herself with sticks like she was doing when she first come. She wasn't laughing much either, but she started playing with the other kids when they come home. Seemed like everybody was working hard to be better with each other.

Come March, Clarissa asks, "Can I dance?"

For sure, the best time for teaching is when a kid wants to listen, so we stood side to side with me doing some steps. She followed along fine. I put on a tape and started moving faster, and Clarissa just kept up all natural. I could tell she'd been practicing lots. She was doing real good.

Comes the next powwow, which was outside on the track field, I braided Clarissa's hair. Did her up with some ermine and bead ties, then give her a purse to carry. It was all beaded with a rose and leaves. Used to be my aunt's. She held it right next to her side with her chin real high. She joined in a Circle dance. I could see she was watching her feet a little and looking how others do their steps, but mostly she was doing wonderful. When Molly Graybull showed up beside her, Clarissa took to a seat and stared. She didn't dance again that night, but I could see there was dreaming coming into her eyes. I saw that fire that said to practice. And she did. I heard her every day in her room. Finally bought her her very own tape recorder so's the rest of us could listen to music too.

Some months passed on. All the kids was getting bigger. Clarissa, she went into the first grade. Harvey went off to community college up in Seattle, and that left me with Ronnie being the oldest at home. Clarissa was keeping herself busy all the time going over to Molly Graybull's. She was coming home with Spider Woman stories and trickster tales. One night she speaks up at supper and says, right clear and loud, "I'm an Assiniboin." Clear as it can be, she says it again. Don't nobody have to say nothing to something that proud said.

Next day I started working on a wing dress for Clarissa. She was going to be needing one for sure real soon.

Comes the first school year powwow and everyone was putting on their best. I called for Clarissa to come to my room. I told her, "I think it's time you have something special for yourself." Then I held up the green satin and saw her eyes full up with glitter. She didn't say nothing. Only kisses me and runs off to her room.

Just as we're all getting out of the car, Clarissa whispered to me, "I'm gonna dance with Molly Graybull." I put my hand on her shoulder to say, "You just listen to your spirit. That's where your music is."

We all danced an Owl dance, a Friendship dance, and a couple of Circle dances. Things was feeling real warm and good, and then it was time for the women's traditional. Clarissa joined the circle. She opened her arms to something nobody but her seemed to hear. That's when I saw that old Eagle woman come down and slide right inside of Clarissa, scooping up that child. There Clarissa was, full up with music. All full with that old, old spirit, letting herself dance through Clarissa's feet. Then Molly Graybull come dancing alongside Clarissa, and they was both the same age.

from

A Gift of Laughter

Allan Sherman

DaddydaddyDADDY!" That's how it came out—one long, excited word. He started yelling it at the top of the stairs, and by the time he bounded into the living room he really had it going good. I'd been talking to his mother about a money problem, and it stopped me mid-sentence.

"Robbie, *please!*" I said. Then I appealed to my wife. "Can't we have just five minutes around here without kids screaming?"

Robbie had been holding something behind his back. Now he swung it around for me to see. "Daddy, *look!*"

It was a picture, drawn in the messy crayon of a seven-year-old. It showed a weird-looking creature with one ear three times as big as the other, one green eye and one red; the head was pear-shaped, and the face needed a shave.

I turned on my son. "Is *that* what you interrupted me for? Couldn't you wait? I'm talking to your mother about something *important!*"

His face clouded up. His eyes filled with bewilderment, rage, then tears. "Awright!" he screamed, and threw the picture to the floor. "But it's *your* birthday Saturday!" Then he ran upstairs.

I looked at the picture on the floor. At the bottom, in

Robbie's careful printing, were some words I hadn't noticed: MY DAD by Robert Sherman.

Just then Robbie slammed the door of his room. But I heard a different door, a door I once slammed—25 years ago—in my grandmother's house in Chicago.

It was the day I heard my grandmother say she needed a *football*. I heard her tell my mother there was going to be a party tonight for the whole family, and she had to have a football, for after supper.

I couldn't imagine *why* Grandmother needed a football. I was sure she wasn't going to play the game with my aunts and uncles.

She had been in America only a few years, and still spoke with a deep Yiddish accent. But Grandma wanted a football, and a football was something in *my* department. If I could get one, I'd be important, a contributor to the party. I slipped out the door.

There were only three footballs in the neighborhood, and they belonged to older kids. Homer Spicer wasn't home. Eddie Polonsky wouldn't sell or rent, at any price.

The last possibility was a tough kid we called Gudgie. It was just as I'd feared. Gudgie punched me in the nose. Then he said he would trade me his old football for my new sled, plus all the marbles I owned.

I filled Gudgie's football with air at the gas station. Then I sneaked it into the house and shined it with shoe polish. When I finished, it was a football worthy of Grandmother's party. All the aunts and uncles would be proud. When nobody was looking I put it on the dining-room table. Then I waited in my room for Grandma to notice it.

But it was Mother who noticed it. "Allan!" she shouted.

I ran to the dining room.

"You know your grandmother's giving a party tonight. Why can't you put your things where they belong?"

"It's not mine," I protested.

"Then give it back to whoever it belongs to. Get it out of here!"

"But it's for Grandma! She said she needed a football for the party." I was holding back the tears.

Mother burst into laughter. "A *football* for the party! Don't you understand your own grandma?" Then, between peals of laughter, Mother explained: "Not football. Fruit bowl! Grandma needs a fruit bowl for the party."

I was starting to cry, so I ran to my room and slammed the door. The worst part of crying was trying to stop. I can still feel it—the shuddering, my breath coming in little, staccato jerks. And each sputtery breath brought back the pain, the frustration, the unwanted feeling that had made me cry in the first place. I was still trying to stop crying when the aunts and uncles arrived. I heard their voices (sounding very far away), and the clink-clink of Grandma's good china, and now and then an explosion of laughter.

After dinner, Mother came in. "Allan," she said, "come with me. I want you to see something." I followed her into the living room.

Grandma was walking around the room like a queen, holding out to each of the aunts and uncles the biggest, most magnificent cut-glass bowl I'd ever seen. There were grapes and bananas in it, red apples, figs and tangerines. And in the center of the bowl, all shiny and brown, was Gudgie's football.

Just then my Uncle Sol offered Grandma a compliment.

"Esther," he said, "that's a beautiful *football*. Real *cott gless*."

Grandma looked at Uncle Sol with great superiority. "Sol," she said, "listen close, you'll learn something. This *cott gless* is called a *frutt boll*, not a *football*. This in the middle, *this* is a *football*."

Uncle Sol was impressed. "Very smot," he said. "Very nice. But, Esther, now tell me something. How come you got a *football* in your *frutt boll?*" He pronounced them both very carefully.

"Because," Grandma said, "today mine Allan brought me a nice present, this football. It's beautiful, no?"

Before Uncle Sol could answer, Grandma continued, "It's beautiful, yess—because from a child is beautiful, anything."

...From a child is beautiful, anything.

I picked up Robbie's picture from the floor. It wasn't bad, at that. One of my ears *is* a little bigger than the other. And usually, when Robbie sees me at the end of the day, I *do* need a shave.

I went up to his room. "Hi, Rob," I said.

His breath was shuddering, and his nose was running. He was packing a cardboard box, as he always does when he Leaves Home. I held up the picture. "Say, I've been looking this over. It's very good."

"I don't care," he said. He threw a comic book into the box and some Erector-set pieces. "Tear it up if you want to. I can't draw, anyhow."

He put on his cap and jacket, picked up the box and walked right past me. I followed him with the picture in my hand.

When he got to the front door, he just stood there, his hand on the knob, the way he always does. I suppose he thinks of the same things I used to, whenever I Left Home. You stand there by the door, and pray *they* won't let you go, because you have no place to go, and if *they* don't want you, who does?

I got my coat and joined him. "Come on," I said. "I'm going with you." And I took him by the hand.

He looked up at me, very scared. "Where we going?"

"The shopping center is open tonight," I said. "We're going to buy a frame for this picture. It's a beautiful picture. We'll hang it in the living room. After we get the frame we're going to have an ice-cream soda and I'll tell you about something."

"About what?"

"Well, you remember that old football your great-grandma keeps in the cut-glass bowl on her dining-room table?"

"Yes."

"Well, I'm going to tell you how she got it."

Rules of the Game

Amy Tan

I was six when my mother taught me the art of invisible strength. It was a strategy for winning arguments, respect from others, and eventually, though neither of us knew it at the time, chess games.

"Bite back your tongue," scolded my mother when I cried loudly, yanking her hand toward the store that sold bags of salted plums. At home, she said, "Wise guy, he not go against wind. In Chinese we say, Come from South, blow with wind—poom!—North will follow. Strongest wind cannot be seen."

The next week I bit back my tongue as we entered the store with the forbidden candies. When my mother finished her shopping, she quietly plucked a small bag of plums from the rack and put it on the counter with the rest of the items.

My mother imparted her daily truths so she could help my older brothers and me rise above our circumstances. We lived in San Francisco's Chinatown. Like most of the other Chinese children who played in the back alleys of restaurants and curio shops, I didn't think we were poor. My bowl was always full, three five-course meals every day, beginning with a soup full of mysterious things I didn't want to know the names of.

We lived on Waverly Place, in a warm, clean, two-bedroom flat that sat above a small Chinese bakery specializing in steamed pastries and dim sum. In the early morning, when the alley was still quiet, I could smell fragrant red beans as they were cooked down to a pasty sweetness. By daybreak, our flat was heavy with the odor of fried sesame balls and sweet curried chicken crescents. From my bed, I would listen as my father got ready for work, then locked the door behind him, one-two-three clicks.

At the end of our two-block alley was a small sandlot playground with swings and slides well-shined down the middle with use. The play area was bordered by wood-slat benches where old-country people sat cracking roasted watermelon seeds with their golden teeth and scattering the husks to an impatient gathering of gurgling pigeons. The best playground, however, was the dark alley itself. It was crammed with daily mysteries and adventures. My brothers and I would peer into the medicinal herb shop, watching old Li dole out onto a stiff sheet of white paper the right amount of insect shells, saffron-colored seeds, and pungent leaves for his ailing customers. It was said that he once cured a woman dying of an ancestral curse that had eluded the best of American doctors. Next to the pharmacy was a printer who specialized in gold-embossed wedding invitations and festive red banners.

Farther down the street was Ping Yuen Fish Market. The front window displayed a tank crowded with doomed fish and turtles struggling to gain footing on the slimy green-tiled sides. A hand-written sign informed tourists, "Within this store, is all for food, not for pet." Inside, the butchers with their bloodstained white smocks deftly gutted the fish while customers cried out their orders and shouted, "Give me your freshest," to which the butchers always protested, "All are freshest." On less crowded market days, we would inspect the crates of live frogs and crabs which we were warned not to poke, boxes of dried cuttlefish, and row upon row of iced prawns, squid, and slippery fish. The sanddabs made me shiver each time; their eyes lay on one flattened side and reminded me of my mother's story of a careless girl who ran into a crowded street and was crushed by a cab. "Was smash flat," reported my mother.

At the corner of the alley was Hong Sing's, a four-table café with a recessed stairwell in front that led to a door marked "Tradesmen." My brothers and I believed the bad people emerged from this door at night. Tourists never went to Hong Sing's, since the menu was printed only in Chinese. A Caucasian man with a big camera once posed me and my playmates in front of the restaurant. He had us move to the side of the picture window so the photo would capture the roasted duck with its head dangling from a juice-covered rope. After he took the picture, I told him he should go into Hong Sing's and eat dinner. When he smiled and asked me what they served, I shouted, "Guts and duck's feet and octopus gizzards!" Then I ran off with my friends, shrieking with laughter as we scampered across the alley and hid in the entryway grotto of the China Gem Company, my heart pounding with hope that he would chase us.

My mother named me after the street that we lived on: Waverly Place Jong, my official name for important American documents. But my family called me Meimei,

"Little Sister." I was the youngest, the only daughter. Each morning before school, my mother would twist and yank on my think black hair until she had formed two tightly wound pigtails. One day, as she struggled to weave a hard-toothed comb through my disobedient hair, I had a sly thought.

I asked her, "Ma, what is Chinese torture?" My mother shook her head. A bobby pin was wedged between her lips. She wetted her palm and smoothed the hair above my ear, then pushed the pin in so that it nicked sharply against my scalp.

"Who say this word?" she asked without a trace of knowing how wicked I was being. I shrugged my shoulders and said, "Some boy in my class said Chinese people do Chinese torture."

"Chinese people do many things," she said simply. "Chinese people do business, do medicine, do painting. Not lazy like American people. We do torture. Best torture."

My older brother Vincent was the one who actually got the chess set. We had gone to the annual Christmas party held at the First Chinese Baptist Church at the end of the alley. The missionary ladies had put together a Santa bag of gifts donated by members of another church. None of the gifts had names on them. There were separate sacks for boys and girls of different ages.

One of the Chinese parishioners had donned a Santa Claus costume and a stiff paper beard with cotton balls glued to it. I think the only children who thought he was the real thing were too young to know that Santa Claus was not Chinese. When my turn came up, the Santa man asked me how old I was. I thought it was a trick question;

I was seven according to the American formula and eight by the Chinese calendar. I said I was born on March 17, 1951. That seemed to satisfy him. He then solemnly asked if I had been a very, very good girl this year and did I believe in Jesus Christ and obey my parents. I knew the only answer to that. I nodded back with equal solemnity.

Having watched the other children opening their gifts, I already knew that the big gifts were not necessarily the nicest ones. One girl my age got a large coloring book of biblical characters, while a less greedy girl who selected a smaller box received a glass vial of lavender toilet water. The sound of the box was also important. A ten-year-old boy had chosen a box that jangled when he shook it. It was a tin globe of the world with a slit for inserting money. He must have thought it was full of dimes and nickels, because when he saw that it had just ten pennies, his face fell with such undisguised disappointment that his mother slapped the side of his head and led him out of the church hall, apologizing to the crowd for her son who had such bad manners he couldn't appreciate such a fine gift.

As I peered into the sack, I quickly fingered the remaining presents, testing their weight, imagining what they contained. I chose a heavy, compact one that was wrapped in shiny silver foil and a red satin ribbon. It was a twelve-pack of Life Savers and I spent the rest of the party arranging and rearranging the candy tubes in the order of my favorites. My brother Winston chose wisely as well. His present turned out to be a box of intricate plastic parts; the instructions on the box proclaimed that when they were properly assembled he would have an authentic miniature replica of a World War II submarine.

Vincent got the chess set, which would have been a very decent present to get at a church Christmas party, except it was obviously used and, as we discovered later, it was missing a black pawn and a white knight. My mother graciously thanked the unknown benefactor, saying, "Too good. Cost too much." At which point, an old lady with fine white, wispy hair nodded toward our family and said with a whistling whisper, "Merry, merry Christmas."

When we got home, my mother told Vincent to throw the chess set away. "She not want it. We not want it, " she said, tossing her head stiffly to the side with a tight, proud smile. My brothers had deaf ears. They were already lining up the chess pieces and reading from the dog-eared instruction book.

I watched Vincent and Winston play during Christmas week. The chessboard seemed to hold elaborate secrets waiting to be untangled. The chessmen were more powerful than old Li's magic herbs that cured ancestral curses. And my brothers wore such serious faces that I was sure something was at stake that was greater than avoiding the tradesmen's door to Hong Sing's.

"Let me! Let me!" I begged between games when one brother or the other would sit back with a deep sigh of relief and victory, the other annoyed, unable to let go of the outcome. Vincent at first refused to let me play, but when I offered my Life Savers as replacements for the buttons that filled in for the missing pieces, he relented. He chose the flavors: wild cherry for the black pawn and peppermint for the white knight. Winner could eat both.

As our mother sprinkled flour and rolled out small doughy circles for the steamed dumplings that would be our dinner that night, Vincent explained the rules, pointing to each piece. "You have sixteen pieces and so do I. One king and queen, two bishops, two knights, two castles, and eight pawns. The pawns can only move forward one step, except on the first move. Then they can move two. But they can only take men by moving crossways like this, except in the beginning, when you can move ahead and take another pawn."

"Why?" I asked as I moved my pawn. "Why can't they move more steps?"

"Because they're pawns," he said.

"But why do they go crossways to take other men? Why aren't there any women and children?"

"Why is the sky blue? Why must you always ask stupid questions?" asked Vincent. "This is a game. These are the rules. I didn't make them up. See. Here. In the book." He jabbed a page with a pawn in his hand. "Pawn. P-A-W-N. Pawn. Read it yourself."

My mother patted the flour off her hands. "Let me see book," she said quietly. She scanned the pages quickly, not reading the foreign English symbols, seeming to search deliberately for nothing in particular.

"This American rules," she concluded at last. "Every time people come out from foreign country, must know rules. You not know, judge say, Too bad, go back. They not telling you why so you can use their way go forward. They say, Don't know why, you find out yourself. But they knowing all the time. Better you take it, find out why yourself." She tossed her head back with a satisfied smile.

I found out about all the whys later. I read the rules and looked up all the big words in a dictionary. I borrowed books from the Chinatown library. I studied each chess piece, trying to absorb the power each contained.

I learned about opening moves and why it's important to control the center early on; the shortest distance between two points is straight down the middle. I learned about the middle game and why tactics between two adversaries are like clashing ideas; the one who plays better has the clearest plans for both attacking and getting out of traps. I learned why it is essential in the endgame to have foresight, a mathematical understanding of all the possible moves, and patience; all weaknesses and advantages become evident to a strong adversary and obscured to a tiring opponent. I discovered that for the whole game one must gather invisible strengths and see the endgame before the game begins.

I also found out why I should never reveal "why" to others. A little knowledge withheld is a great advantage one should store for future use. That is the power of chess. It is a game of secrets in which one must show and never tell.

I loved the secrets I found within the sixty-four black and white squares. I carefully drew a handmade chessboard and pinned it to the wall next to my bed, where at night I would stare for hours at imaginary battles. Soon I no longer lost my games or Life Savers, but I lost my adversaries. Winston and Vincent decided they were more interested in roaming the streets after school in their Hopalong Cassidy cowboy hats.

On a cold spring afternoon, while walking home from school, I detoured through the playground at the end of our alley. I saw a group of old men, two seated across a folding table playing a game of chess, others smoking pipes, eating peanuts, and watching. I ran home and grabbed Vincent's chess set, which was bound in a cardboard box with rubber bands. I also carefully selected two prized rolls of Life Savers. I can back to the park and approached a man who was observing the game.

"Want to play?" I asked him. His face widened with surprise and he grinned as he looked at the box under my arm.

"Little sister, been a long time since I play with dolls," he said, smiling benevolently. I quickly put the box down next to him on the bench and displayed my retort.

Lau Po, as he allowed me to call him, turned out to be a much better player than my brothers. I lost many games and many Life Savers. But over the weeks, with each diminishing roll of candies, I added new secrets. Lau Po gave me the names. The Double Attack from the East and West Shores. Throwing Stones on the Drowning Man. The Sudden Meeting of the Clan. The Surprise from the Sleeping Guard. The Humble Servant Who Kills the King. Sand in the Eyes of Advancing Forces. A Double Killing Without Blood.

There were also the fine points of chess etiquette. Keep captured men in neat rows, as well-tended prisoners. Never announce "Check" with vanity, lest someone with an unseen sword slit your throat. Never hurl pieces into the sandbox after you have lost a game, because then you must find them again, by yourself, after apologizing to all around you. By the end of the summer, Lau Po had taught me all he knew, and I had become a better chess player.

A small weekend crowd of Chinese people and tourists would gather as I played and defeated my opponents one by one. My mother would join the crowds during these outdoor exhibition games. She sat proudly on the bench, telling my admirers with proper Chinese humility, "Is luck."

A man who watched me play in the park suggested that my mother allow me to play in local chess tournaments. My mother smiled graciously, an answer that meant nothing. I desperately wanted to go, but I bit back my tongue. I knew she would not let me play among strangers. So as we walked home I said in a small voice that I didn't want to play in the local tournament. They would have American rules. If I lost, I would bring shame on my family.

"Is shame you fall down nobody push you," said my mother.

During my first tournament, my mother sat with me in the front row as I waited for my turn. I frequently bounced my legs to unstick them from the cold metal seat of the folding chair. When my name was called, I leapt up. My mother unwrapped something in her lap. It was her *chang*, a small tablet of red jade which held the sun's fire. "Is luck," she whispered, and tucked it into my dress pocket. I turned to my opponent, a fifteen-year-old boy from Oakland. He looked at me, wrinkling his nose.

As I began to play, the boy disappeared, the color ran out of the room, and I saw only my white pieces and his black ones waiting on the other side. A light wind began blowing past my ears. It whispered secrets only I could hear.

"Blow from the South," it murmured. "The wind leaves no trail." I saw a clear path, the traps to avoid. The crowd rustled. "Shhh! Shhh!" said the corners of the room. The wind blew stronger. "Throw sand from the East to distract him." The knight came forward ready for the sacrifice. The wind hissed, louder and louder. "Blow, blow, blow. He cannot see. He is blind now. Make him lean away from the wind so he is easier to knock down."

"Check," I said, as the wind roared with laughter. The wind died down to little puffs, my own breath.

My mother placed my first trophy next to a new plastic chess set that the neighborhood Tao society had given to me. As she wiped each piece with a soft cloth, she said, "Next time win more, lose less."

"Ma, it's not how many pieces you lose," I said. "Sometimes you need to lose pieces to get ahead."

"Better to lose less, see if you really need."

At the next tournament, I won again, but it was my mother who wore the triumphant grin.

"Lost eight piece this time. Last time was eleven. What I tell you? Better off lose less!" I was annoyed, but I couldn't say anything.

I attended more tournaments, each one farther away from home. I won all games, in all divisions. The Chinese bakery downstairs from our flat displayed my growing collection of trophies in its window, amidst the dust-covered cakes that were never picked up. The day after I won an important regional tournament, the window encased a fresh sheet cake with whipped-cream frosting and red script saying "Congratulations, Waverly Jong, Chinatown Chess Champion." Soon after that, a flower shop, headstone engraver, and funeral parlor offered to sponsor me in national tournaments. That's when my mother decided that I no longer had to do the dishes. Winston and Vincent had to do my chores.

"Why does she get to play and we do all the work," complained Vincent.

"Is new American rules," said my mother. "Meimei play, squeeze all her brains out for win chess. You play, worth squeeze towel."

By my ninth birthday, I was a national chess champion. I was still some 429 points away from grand-master status, but I was touted as the Great American Hope, a child prodigy and a girl to boot. They ran a photo of me in *Life* magazine next to a quote in which Bobby Fischer said, "There will never be a woman grand master." "Your move, Bobby," said the caption.

The day they took the magazine picture I wore neatly plaited braids clipped with plastic barrettes trimmed with rhinestones. I was playing in a large high school auditorium that echoed with phlegmy coughs and the squeaky rubber knobs of chair legs sliding across freshly waxed wooden floors. Seated across from me was an American man, about the same age as Lau Po, maybe fifty. I remember that his sweaty brow seemed to weep at my every move. He wore a dark, malodorous suit. One of his pockets was stuffed with a great white kerchief on which he wiped his palm before sweeping his hand over the chosen chess piece with great flourish.

In my crisp pink-and-white dress with scratchy lace at the neck, one of two my mother had sewn for these special occasions, I would clasp my hands under my chin, the delicate points of my elbows poised lightly on the table in the manner my mother had shown me for posing for the press. I would swing my patent leather shoes back and forth like an impatient child riding on a school bus. Then I would pause, suck in my lips, twirl my chosen piece in midair as

if undecided, and then firmly plant it in its new threat-
ening place, with a triumphant smile thrown back at my
opponent for good measure.

I no longer played in the alley of Waverly Place. I never
visited the playground where the pigeons and old men
gathered. I went to school, then directly home to learn
new chess secrets, cleverly concealed advantages, more
escape routes.

But I found it difficult to concentrate at home. My
mother had a habit of standing over me while I plotted out
my games. I think she thought of herself as my protective
ally. Her lips would be sealed tight, and after each move I
made, a soft "Hmmmmph" would escape from her nose.

"Ma, I can't practice when you stand there like that,"
I said one day. She retreated to the kitchen and made loud
noises with the pots and pans. When the crashing stopped,
I could see out of the corner of my eye that she was
standing in the doorway. "Hmmmph!" Only this one came
out of her tight throat.

My parents made many concessions to allow me to
practice. One time I complained that the bedroom I shared
was so noisy that I couldn't think. Thereafter, my brothers
slept in a bed in the living room facing the street. I said I
couldn't finish my rice; my head didn't work right when my
stomach was too full. I left the table with half-finished
bowls and nobody complained. But there was one duty I
couldn't avoid. I had to accompany my mother on Saturday market days when I had no tournament to play. My
mother would proudly walk with me, visiting many shops,
buying very little. "This my daughter Wave-ly Jong," she
said to whoever looked her way.

One day after we left a shop I said under my breath, "I wish you wouldn't do that, telling everybody I'm your daughter." My mother stopped walking. Crowds of people with heavy bags pushed past us on the sidewalk, bumping into first one shoulder, then another.

"Aiii-ya. So shame be with mother?" She grasped my hand even tighter as she glared at me.

I looked down. "It's not that, it's just so obvious. It's just so embarrassing."

"Embarrass you be my daughter?" Her voice was cracking with anger.

"That's not what I meant. That's not what I said."

"What you say?"

I knew it was a mistake to say anything more, but I heard my voice speaking, "Why do you have to use me to show off? If you want to show off, then why don't you learn to play chess?"

My mother's eyes turned into dangerous black slits. She had no words for me, just sharp silence.

I felt the wind rushing around my hot ears. I jerked my hand out of my mother's tight grasp and spun around, knocking into an old woman. Her bag of groceries spilled to the ground.

"Aii-ya! Stupid girl!" my mother and the woman cried. Oranges and tin cans careened down the sidewalk. As my mother stooped to help the old woman pick up the escaping food, I took off.

I raced down the street, dashing between people, not looking back as my mother screamed shrilly, "Meimei! Meimei!" I fled down an alley, past dark, curtained shops and merchants washing the grime off their windows. I sped into the sunlight, into a large street crowded with tourists examining trinkets and souvenirs. I ducked into another dark alley, down another street, up another alley. I ran until it hurt and I realized I had nowhere to go, that I was not running from anything. The alleys contained no escape routes.

My breath came out like angry smoke. It was cold. I sat down on an upturned plastic pail next to a stack of empty boxes, cupping my chin with my hands, thinking hard. I imagined my mother, first walking briskly down one street or another looking for me, then giving up and returning home to await my arrival. After two hours, I stood up on creaking legs and slowly walked home.

The alley was quiet and I could see the yellow lights shining from our flat like two tiger's eyes in the night. I climbed the sixteen steps to the door, advancing quietly up each so as not to make any warning sounds. I turned the knob; the door was locked. I heard a chair moving, quick steps, the locks turning—click! click! click!—and then the door opened.

"About time you got home," said Vincent. "Boy, are you in trouble."

He slid back to the dinner table. On a platter were the remains of a large fish, its fleshy head still connected to bones swimming upstream in vain escape. Standing there waiting for my punishment, I heard my mother speak in a dry voice.

"We not concerning this girl. This girl not have concerning for us."

Nobody looked at me. Bone chopsticks clinked against the insides of bowls being emptied into hungry mouths.

I walked into my room, closed the door, and lay down on my bed. The room was dark, the ceiling filled with shadows from the dinnertime lights of neighboring flats.

In my head, I saw a chessboard with sixty-four black and white squares. Opposite me was my opponent, two angry black slits. She wore a triumphant smile. "Strongest wind cannot be seen," she said.

Her black men advanced across the plane, slowly marching to each successive level as a single unit. My white pieces screamed as they scurried and fell off the board one by one. As her men drew closer to my edge, I felt myself growing light. I rose up into the air and flew out the window. Higher and higher, above the alley, over the tops of tiled roofs, where I was gathered up by the wind and pushed up toward the night sky until everything below me disappeared and I was alone.

I closed my eyes and pondered my next move.

The Circuit

Francisco Jiménez

It was that time of year again. Ito, the strawberry share-cropper, did not smile. It was natural. The peak of the strawberry season was over and the last few days the work-ers, most of them braceros, were not picking as many boxes as they had during the months of June and July.

As the last days of August disappeared, so did the number of braceros. Sunday, only one—the best picker—came to work. I liked him. Sometimes we talked during our half-hour lunch break. That is how I found out he was from Jalisco, the same state in Mexico my family was from. That Sunday was the last time I saw him.

When the sun had tired and sunk behind the moun-tains, Ito signaled us that it was time to go home. "Ya esora," he yelled in his broken Spanish. Those were the words I waited for twelve hours a day, every day, seven days a week, week after week. And the thought of not hearing them again saddened me.

As we drove home Papá did not say a word. With both hands on the wheel, he stared at the dirt road. My older brother, Roberto, was also silent. He leaned his head back and closed his eyes. Once in a while he cleared from his throat the dust that blew in from outside.

Yes, it was that time of year. When I opened the front door to the shack, I stopped. Everything we owned was neatly packed in cardboard boxes. Suddenly I felt even more the weight of hours, days, weeks, and months of work. I sat down on a box. The thought of having to move to Fresno and knowing what was in store for me there brought tears to my eyes.

That night I could not sleep. I lay in bed thinking about how much I hated this move.

A little before five o'clock in the morning, Papá woke everyone up. A few minutes later, the yelling and screaming of my little brothers and sisters, for whom the move was a great adventure, broke the silence of dawn. Shortly, the barking of the dogs accompanied them.

While we packed the breakfast dishes, Papá went outside to start the "Carcanchita." That was the name Papá gave his old '38 black Plymouth. He bought it in a used-car lot in Santa Rosa in the winter of 1949. Papá was very proud of his little jalopy. He had a right to be proud of it. He spent a lot of time looking at other cars before buying this one. When he finally chose the "Carcanchita," he checked it thoroughly before driving it out of the car lot. He examined every inch of the car. He listened to the motor, tilting his head from side to side like a parrot, trying to detect any noises that spelled car trouble. After being satisfied with the looks and sounds of the car, Papá then insisted on knowing who the original owner was. He never did find out from the car salesman, but he bought the car anyway. Papá figured the original owner must have been an important man because behind the rear seat of the car he found a blue necktie.

Papá parked the car out in front and left the motor

running. "Listo," he yelled. Without saying a word, Roberto and I began to carry the boxes out to the car. Roberto carried the two big boxes and I carried the two smaller ones. Papá then threw the mattress on top of the car roof and tied it with ropes to the front and rear bumpers.

Everything was packed except Mamá's pot. It was an old large galvanized pot she had picked up at an army surplus store in Santa María the year I was born. The pot had many dents and nicks, and the more dents and nicks it acquired the more Mamá liked it. "Mi olla," she used to say proudly.

I held the front door open as Mamá carefully carried out her pot by both handles, making sure not to spill the cooked beans. When she got to the car, Papá reached out to help her with it. Roberto opened the rear car door and Papá gently placed it on the floor behind the front seat. All of us then climbed in. Papá sighed, wiped the sweat off his forehead with his sleeve, and said wearily: "Es todo."

As we drove away, I felt a lump in my throat. I turned around and looked at our little shack for the last time.

At sunset we drove into a labor camp near Fresno. Since Papá did not speak English, Mamá asked the camp foreman if he needed any more workers. "We don't need no more," said the foreman, scratching his head. "Check with Sullivan down the road. Can't miss him. He lives in a big white house with a fence around it."

When we got there, Mamá walked up to the house. She went through a white gate, past a row of rose bushes, up the stairs to the front door. She rang the doorbell. The porch light went on and a tall husky man came out. They exchanged a few words. After the man went in, Mamá clasped her hands and hurried back to the car. "We have work! Mr. Sullivan said we can stay there the whole season," she said, gasping and pointing to an old garage near the stables.

The garage was worn out by the years. It had no windows. The walls, eaten by termites, strained to support the roof full of holes. The dirt floor, populated by earth worms, looked like a gray road map.

That night, by the light of a kerosene lamp, we unpacked and cleaned our new home. Roberto swept away the loose dirt, leaving the hard ground. Papá plugged the holes in the walls with old newspapers and tin can tops. Mamá fed my little brothers and sisters. Papá and Roberto then brought in the mattress and placed it on the far corner of the garage. "Mamá, you and the little ones sleep on the mattress. Roberto, Panchito, and I will sleep outside under the trees," Papá said.

Early next morning Mr. Sullivan showed us where his crop was, and after breakfast, Papá, Roberto, and I headed for the vineyard to pick.

Around nine o'clock the temperature had risen to almost one hundred degrees. I was completely soaked in sweat and my mouth felt as if I had been chewing on a handkerchief. I walked over to the end of the row, picked up the jug of water we had brought, and began drinking. "Don't drink too much; you'll get sick," Roberto shouted. No sooner had he said that then I felt sick to my stomach. I dropped to my knees and let the jug roll off my hands. I remained motionless with my eyes glued on the hot sandy ground. All I could hear was the drone of insects. Slowly I began to recover. I poured water over my face and neck and watched the dirty water run down my arms to the ground.

I still felt a little dizzy when we took a break to eat lunch. It was past two o'clock and we sat underneath a large walnut tree that was on the side of the road. While we ate, Papá jotted down the number of boxes we had picked. Roberto drew designs on the ground with a stick. Suddenly I noticed Papá's face turn pale as he looked down the road. "Here comes the school bus," he whispered loudly in alarm. Instinctively, Roberto and I ran and hid in the vineyards. We did not want to get in trouble for not going to school. The neatly dressed boys about my age got off. They carried books under their arms. After they crossed the street, the bus drove away. Roberto and I came out from hiding and joined Papá. "Tienen que tener cuidado," he warned us.

After lunch we went back to work. The sun kept beating down. The buzzing insects, the wet sweat, and the hot dry dust made the afternoon seem to last forever. Finally the mountains around the valley reached out and swallowed the sun. Within an hour it was too dark to continue picking. The vines blanketed the grapes, making it difficult to see the bunches. "Vámonos," said Papá, signaling to us that it was time to quit work. Papá then took out a pencil and began to figure out how much we had earned our first day. He wrote down numbers, crossed some out, wrote down some more. "Quince," he murmured.

When we arrived home, we took a cold shower underneath a waterhose. We then sat down to eat dinner around some wooden crates that served as a table. Mamá had cooked a special meal for us. We had rice and tortillas with "carne con chile," my favorite dish.

The next morning I could hardly move. My body ached all over. I felt little control over my arms and legs.

This feeling went on every morning for days until my muscles finally got used to the work.

It was Monday, the first week of November. The grape season was over and I could now go to school. I woke up early that morning and lay in bed, looking at the stars and savoring the thought of not going to work and of starting sixth grade for the first time that year. Since I could not sleep, I decided to get up and join Papá and Roberto at breakfast. I sat at the table across from Roberto, but I kept my head down. I did not want to look up and face him. I knew he was sad. He was not going to school today. He was not going tomorrow, or next week, or next month. He would not go until the cotton season was over, and that was sometime in February. I rubbed my hands together and watched the dry, acid-stained skin fall to the floor in little rolls.

When Papá and Roberto left for work, I felt relief. I walked to the top of a small grade next to the shack and watched the "Carcanchita" disappear in the distance in a cloud of dust.

Two hours later, around eight o'clock, I stood by the side of the road waiting for school bus number twenty. When it arrived I climbed in. Everyone was busy either talking or yelling. I sat in an empty seat in the back.

When the bus stopped in front of the school, I felt very nervous. I looked out the bus window and saw boys and girls carrying books under their arms. I put my hands in my pant pockets and walked to the principal's office. When I entered I heard a woman's voice say: "May I help you?" I was startled. I had not heard English for months. For a few seconds I remained speechless. I looked at the lady who waited for an answer. My first instinct was to answer her in

Spanish, but I held back. Finally, after struggling for English words, I managed to tell her that I wanted to enroll in the sixth grade. After answering many questions, I was led to the classroom.

Mr. Lema, the sixth grade teacher, greeted me and assigned me a desk. He then introduced me to the class. I was so nervous and scared at that moment when everyone's eyes were on me that I wished I were with Papá and Roberto picking cotton. After taking roll, Mr. Lema gave the class the assignment for the first hour. "The first thing we have to do this morning is finish reading the story we began yesterday," he said enthusiastically. He walked up to me, handed me an English book, and asked me to read. "We are on page 125," he said politely. When I heard this, I felt my blood rush to my head; I felt dizzy. "Would you like to read?" he asked hesitantly. I opened the book to page 125. My mouth was dry. My eyes began to water. I could not begin. "You can read later," Mr. Lema said understandingly.

For the rest of the reading period I kept getting angrier and angrier with myself. I should have read, I thought to myself.

During recess I went into the restroom and opened my English book to page 125. I began to read in a low voice, pretending I was in class. There were many words I did not know. I closed the book and headed back to the classroom.

Mr. Lema was sitting at his desk correcting papers. When I entered he looked up at me and smiled. I felt better. I walked up to him and asked if he could help me with the new words. "Gladly," he said.

The rest of the month I spent my lunch hours working on English with Mr. Lema, my best friend at school.

One Friday during lunch hour Mr. Lema asked me to take a walk with him to the music room. "Do you like music?" he asked me as we entered the building.

"Yes, I like corridos," I answered. He then picked up a trumpet, blew on it, and handed it to me. The sound gave me goose bumps. I knew that sound. I had heard it in many corridos. "How would you like to learn how to play it?" he asked. He must have read my face because before I could answer, he added, "I'll teach you how to play it during our lunch hours."

That day I could hardly wait to get home to tell Papá and Mamá the great news. As I got off the bus, my little brothers and sisters ran up to meet me. They were yelling and screaming. I thought they were happy to see me, but when I opened the door to our shack, I saw that everything we owned was neatly packed in cardboard boxes.

Bad Influence

Judith Ortiz Cofer

When I was sent to spend the summer at my grandparents' house in Puerto Rico, I knew it was going to be strange, I just didn't know how strange. My parents insisted that I was going to go either to a Catholic girls' retreat or to my mother's folks on the island. Some choice. It was either breakfast, lunch, and dinner with the Sisters of Charity in a convent somewhere in the woods—far from beautiful downtown Paterson, New Jersey, where I really wanted to spend my summer—or *arroz y habichuelas* with the old people in the countryside of my parents' island.

My whole life, I had seen my grandparents only once a year when we went down for a two-week vacation, and frankly, I spent all my time at the beach with my cousins and let the adults sit around drinking their hot *café con leche* and sweating, gossiping about people I didn't know. This time there would be no cousins to hang around with—vacation time for the rest of the family was almost three months away. It was going to be a long hot summer.

Did I say hot? When I stepped off that airplane in San Juan, it was like I had opened an oven door. I was immediately drenched in sweat, and felt like I was breathing water.

To make matters worse, there were Papá Juan, Mamá Ana, and about a dozen other people waiting to hug me and ask me a million questions in Spanish—not my best language. The others were *vecinos*, neighbors who had nothing better to do than come to the airport to pick me up in a caravan of cars. My friends from Central High would have died laughing if they had seen the women with their fans going back and forth across their shiny faces fighting over who was going to take my bags, and who was going to sit next to whom in the cars for the fifteen-minute drive home. Someone put a chubby brown baby on my lap, and even though I tried to ignore her, she curled up around me like a koala bear and went to sleep. I felt her little chest going up and down and I made my breath match hers. I sat in the back of Papá Juan's *un*-air-conditioned *sub*compact in between Doña This and Doña That, practicing Zen. I had been reading about it in a magazine on the airplane, about how to lower your blood pressure by concentrating on your breathing, so I decided to give it a try. My grandmother turned around with a worried look on her face and said, "Rita, do you have asthma? Your mother didn't tell me."

Before I could say anything, everybody in the car started talking at once, telling asthma stories. I continued to take deep breaths, but it didn't help. By the time we got to Mamá Ana's house, I had a pounding headache. I excused myself from my welcoming committee, handed the damp baby (she was really cute) over to her grandmother, and went to lie down in the room where Papá Juan had put my bags.

Of course, there was no AC. The window was thrown wide open, and right outside, perched on a fence separating our house from the neighbors' by about six inches, there was a red rooster. When I looked at him, he started screeching at the top of his lungs. I closed the window, but I could still hear him crowing; then someone turned on a radio, *loud*. I put a pillow over my head and decided to commit suicide by sweating to death. I must have dozed off, because when I opened my eyes, I saw my grandfather sitting on a chair outside my window, which had been opened again. He was stroking the rooster's feathers and seemed to be whispering something in his ear. He finally noticed me sitting in a daze on the edge of my four-poster bed, which was about ten feet off the ground.

"You were dreaming about your boyfriend," he said to me. "It was not a pleasant dream. No, I don't think it was *muy bueno*."

Great. My mother hadn't told me that her father had gone senile. But I *had* been dreaming about Johnny Ruiz, one of the reasons I had been sent away for the summer. Just a coincidence, I decided. But what about privacy? Had I or had I not closed the window in my room?

"Papá," I said assertively, "I think we need to talk."

"There is no need to talk when you can see into people's hearts," he said, setting the rooster on my window ledge. "This is Ramón. He is a good rooster and makes the hens happy and productive, but Ramón has a little problem that you will soon notice. He cannot tell time very accurately. To him, day is night and night is day. It is all the same to him, and when the spirit moves him, he sings. This is not a bad thing in itself, *entiendes?* But it sometimes annoys people. *Entonces*, I have to come and calm him down."

I could not believe what I was hearing. It was like I was in a *Star Trek* rerun where reality is being controlled by an alien, and you don't know why weird things are happening all around you until the end of the show.

Ramón jumped into my room and up on my bed, where he spread his wings and crowed like a madman.

"He is welcoming you to Puerto Rico," my grandfather said. I decided to go sit in the living room.

"I have prepared you a special tea for your asthma." Mamá Ana came in carrying a cup of some foul-smelling green stuff.

"I don't have asthma," I tried to explain. But she had already set the cup in my hands and was on her way to the TV.

"My *telenovela* comes on at this hour," she announced.

Mamá Ana turned the volume way up as the theme music came on, with violins wailing like cats mating. I had always suspected that all my Puerto Rican relatives were a little bit deaf. She sat in a rocking chair right next to the sofa where I was lying down. I was still feeling like a wet noodle from the heat.

"Drink your *guarapo* while it's still hot," she insisted, her eyes glued to the TV screen, where a girl was crying about something.

"*Pobrecita,*" my grandmother said sadly, "her miserable husband left her without a penny, and she's got three little children and one on the way."

"Oh, God," I groaned. It was really going to be *The Twilight Zone* around here. Neither one of the old guys could tell the difference between fantasy and reality—Papá with his dream-reading and Mamá with her telenovelas. I had to call my mother and tell her that I had changed my mind about the convent.

I was going to have to locate a telephone first, though—AT&T had not yet sold my grandparents on the concept of high-tech communications. Letters were still good enough for them, and a telegram when someone died. The nearest phone was at the house of a neighbor, a nice fat woman who watched you while you talked. I had tried calling a friend last summer from her house. There had been a conversation going on in the same room where I was using the phone, a running commentary on what I was saying in English as understood by her granddaughter. They had both thought that eavesdropping on me was a good way to practice their English. My mother had explained that it was not malicious. It was just that people on the island did not see as much need for privacy as people who lived on the mainland. "Puerto Ricans are friendlier. Keeping secrets among friends is considered offensive," she had told me.

My grandmother explained the suffering woman's problems in the telenovela. She'd had to get married because the man she loved was a villain who had forced her to prove her love for him. "*Tú sabes como*. You know how." Then he had kept her practically a prisoner, isolated from her own *familia*. Ay, *bendito*, my grandmother exclaimed as the evil husband came home and started demanding food on the table and a fresh suit of clothes. He was going out, he said, with *los muchachos*. *Pero no*. My grandmother knew better than that. He had another woman. She was sure of it. She spoke to the crying woman on the TV: "*Mira*," she advised her, "open your eyes and see what is going on. For the sake of your children. Leave this man. Go back home to your *mamá*. She's a good woman, although you have hurt her, and she is ill. Perhaps with cancer. But she will take you and the children back."

"Ohhh," I moaned.

"Sit up and drink your tea, Rita. If you're not better by

tomorrow, I'll have to take you to my *comadre*. She makes the best herbal laxatives on the island. People come from all over to buy them—because what ails most people is a clogged system. You clean it out like a pipe, entiendes? You flush it out and then you feel good again."

"I'm going to bed," I announced, even though it was only nine—hours before my usual bedtime. I could hear Ramón crowing from the direction of my bedroom.

"It's a good idea to get some rest tonight, *hija*. Tomorrow Juan has to do a job out by the beach, a woman whose daughter won't eat or get out of bed. They think it is a spiritual matter. You and I will go with him. I have a craving for crab meat, and we can pick some up."

"Pick some up?"

"*Sí*, when the crabs crawl out of their holes and into our traps. We'll take some pots and boil them on the beach. They'll be *sabrosos*."

"I'm going to bed now," I repeated like a zombie. I took a running start from the door and jumped on the bed with all my clothes on. Outside my window, Ramón crowed; the neighbor woman called out, "Ana, Ana, do you think she'll leave him?" while my grandmother yelled back, "No. *Pienso que no*. She's a fool for love, that one is."

I shut my eyes and tried to fly back to my room at home. When I had my own telephone, I could sometimes sneak a call to Johnny late at night. He had basketball practice every afternoon, so we couldn't talk earlier. I was desperate to be with him. He was on the varsity team at Eastside High and a very popular guy. That's how we met: at a game. I had gone with my friend Meli from Central because her boyfriend played for

Eastside, too. He was an Anglo, though. Actually, he was Italian but looked Puerto Rican. Neither of the guys was exactly into meeting parents, and our folks didn't let us go out with anybody whose total ancestry they didn't know, so Meli and I had to sneak out and meet them after games.

Dating is not a concept adults in our barrio really "get." It's supposed to be that a girl meets a guy from the neighborhood, and their parents went to school together, and everybody knows everybody's business. But Meli and I were doing all right until Joey and Johnny asked us to spend the night in Joey's house. The Molieris had gone out of town and we would have the place to ourselves. Meli and I talked about it constantly for days, until we came up with a plan. It was risky, but we thought we could get away with it. We each said we were spending the night at the other's house. We'd done it a lot of times before, and our mothers never checked on us. They just told us to call if anything went wrong. Well, it turned out Meli's mom got a case of heartburn that she thought was a heart attack, and her husband called our house. She almost did have one for real when she found out Meli wasn't there. They called the cops, and woke up everybody they thought we knew. When Meli's little sister cracked under pressure and mentioned Joey Molieri, all four of them drove over to West Paterson at 2:00 A.M. and pounded on the door like crazy people. The guys thought it was a drug bust. But I knew, and when I looked at Meli and saw the look of terror on her face, I knew she knew what we were in for.

We were put under house arrest after that, not even allowed to make phone calls, which I think is against the law. Anyway, it was a mess. That's when I was given the two choices for my summer. And naturally I picked the winner—spending three months with two batty old people and one demented rooster.

The worst part is that I didn't deserve it. My mother interrogated me about what had happened between me and *that boy*, as she called him. Nothing. I admit that I was thinking about it. Johnny had told me that he liked me and wanted to take me out, but he usually dated older girls and he expected them to have sex with him. Apparently, he and Joey had practiced their speeches together, because Meli and I compared notes in the bathroom at one point, and she had heard the same thing from him.

But our parents had descended on us while we were still discussing it. Would I do it? To have a boyfriend like Johnny Ruiz? He can go out with any girl, white, black, or Puerto Rican. But he says I'm mature for almost fifteen. After the mess, I snuck a call to him one night when my mother had forgotten to unplug the phone and lock it up like she'd been doing whenever she had to leave me alone in the apartment. Johnny said he thinks my parents are nuts, but he's willing to give me another chance when I come back in the fall.

"We'll be getting up real early tomorrow." My grandmother was at my door. Barged in without knocking, of course. "We'll be up with the chickens, so we can catch the crabs when the sun brings them out. *Está bien?*" Then she came to sit on my bed, which took some doing, since it was almost as tall as she.

"I am glad that you are here, *mi niña*." She grabbed my head and kissed me hard on my cheek. She smelled like coffee with boiled milk and sugar, which the natives drink by the gallon in spite of the heat. I was thinking that my grandmother didn't remember that I was almost fifteen years old and I would have to remind her.

But then she got serious and said to me, "I was your age when I met Juan. I married him a year later and started having babies. They're scattered all over *los Estados Unidos* now. Did I ever tell you that I wanted to be a professional dancer? At your age I was winning contests and traveling with a mambo band. Do you dance, Rita? You should, *sabes?* It's hard to be unhappy when your feet are moving to music."

I was more than a little surprised by what Mamá Ana said about wanting to be a dancer and marrying at fifteen, and wouldn't have minded hearing more, but then Papá Juan came into my room too. I guessed it was going to be a party, so I sat up and turned on the light.

"Where is my bottle of holy water, Ana?" he asked.

"On the altar in our room, *señor*," she replied, "where it always is."

Of course, I thought, the holy water was on the altar, where everybody keeps their holy water. I must have made a funny noise, because both of them turned their eyes to me, looking very concerned.

"Is it that asthma again, Rita?" My grandmother felt my forehead. "I noticed you didn't finish your tea. I'll go make you some more as soon as I help your *abuelo* find his things for tomorrow."

"I'm not sick. Please. Just a little tired," I said firmly, hoping to get my message across. But I had to know. "What is it he's going to do tomorrow, exorcise demons out of somebody, or what?"

They looked at each other then as if *I* was crazy.

"You explain it to her, Ana," he said. "I have to prepare myself for this *trabajo*."

My grandmother came back to the bed, climbed up on
it, and began telling me how Papá was a medium, a spiri-
tist. He had special gifts, *facultades*, which he had discovered as a young man, that allowed him to see into people's
hearts and minds through prayers and in dreams.

"Does he sacrifice chickens and goats?" I had heard
about these voodoo priests who went into trances and
poured blood and feathers all over everybody in secret cer-
emonies. There was a black man from Haiti in our neighborhood who people said could even call back the dead and
make them his zombie slaves. There was always a dare on
to go to his door on some excuse and try to see what was in
his basement apartment, but nobody I knew had ever done
it. What had my own mother sent me into? I would probably be sent back to Paterson as one of the walking dead.

"No, *Dios mío*, no!" Mamá Ana shouted, and crossed
herself and kissed the cross on her neck chain. "Your
grandfather works with God and His saints, not with
Satan!"

"Excuse *me*," I said, thinking that I really should have
been given an instruction manual before being sent here
on my own.

"Tomorrow you will see how Juan helps people. This
muchacha that he has been summoned to work on has
stopped eating. She does not want to speak to her mother,
who is the one who called us. Your grandfather will see
what is making her spirit sick."

"Why don't they take her to a . . ." I didn't know the
word for shrink in Spanish, so I just said, "to a doctor for
crazy people."

"Because not everyone who is sad or troubled is crazy. If it is their brain that is sick, that is one thing, but if it is their soul that is in pain—then Juan can sometimes help. He can contact the guides, that is, spirits who are concerned about the ailing person, and they can sometimes show him what needs to be done. ¿Entiendes?"

"Uh-huh," I said.

She planted another smack on my face and left to help her husband pack his Ghostbuster equipment. I finally fell asleep thinking about Johnny and what it would be like to be his girlfriend.

"Getting up with the chickens" meant that both my grandparents were up and talking at the top of their lungs by about four in the morning. I put my head under the sheet and hoped that my presence in their house had slipped their minds. No luck. Mamá Ana came into my room, turned on the overhead light, and pulled down the sheet. It had been years since my own parents had dared to barge into my bedroom. I would have been furious, except I was so sleepy I couldn't build up to it, so I just curled up and decided it was time to use certain things to my advantage.

"Ohhh . . ." I moaned and gasped for air.

"Hija, what is wrong?" Mamá sounded so worried that I almost gave up my little plan.

"It's my asthma, Mamá," I said in a weak voice. "I guess all the excitement is making it act up. I'll just take my medicine and stay in bed today."

"*Positivamente no!*" she said, putting a hand that smelled of mint from her garden on my forehead. "I will stay with you and have my comadre come over. She will prepare you a tea that will clear your system like—"

"Like a clogged sewer pipe." I completed the sentence

for her. "No, I'll go with you. I'm feeling better now."

"Are you sure, Rita? You are more important to me than any poor girl sick in her soul. And I don't need to eat crab, either. Once in a while I get these *antojos*, you know, whims, like a pregnant woman, ha, ha. But they pass."

Somehow we got out of the house before the sun came up and sandwiched ourselves into the subcompact, whose muffler must have woken up half the island. Why doesn't anyone ever mention noise pollution around here? was my last thought before I fell asleep crunched up in the backseat.

When I opened my eyes, I was blinded by the glare of the sun coming through the car windows; and when my eyeballs came back into their sockets, I saw that we had pulled up at the side of a house right on the beach. This was no ordinary house. It looked like a huge pink-and-white birthday cake. No joke—it was painted baby pink with white trim and a white roof. It had a terrace that went all the way around it, so that it really did look like a layer cake. If I could afford a house like that, I would paint it a more serious color. Like purple. But around here, everyone is crazy about pastels: lime green, baby pink and blue—nursery school colors.

The ocean was incredible, though. It was just a few yards away and it looked unreal. The water was turquoise in some places and dark blue, almost black, in others—I guessed those were the deep spots. I had been left alone in the car, so I looked around to see if the old people were anywhere in sight. I saw my grandmother first, off on the far left side of the beach where it started to curve, up to her knees in water, dragging something by a rope. Catching crabs, I guessed. I needed to stretch, so I walked over to where she was. Although the sun was a little white ball in the sky, it wasn't unbearably hot yet. In fact, with the breeze blowing, it was almost perfect. I wondered if I could get them to leave me here. Then I remembered the "job" my grandfather had come to do. I glanced up at the top layer of the cake, where I thought the bedroom would be— to see if anything was flying out of the windows. Morning was a strange time for weird stuff, but no matter how hard I tried, I couldn't feel down about anything right then. It was so sunny, and the whole beach was empty except for one old lady out there violating the civil rights of sea creatures, and me.

"Mira, mira!" Mamá Ana yelled, pulling a cagelike box out of the water. Claws stuck through the slats, snapping like scissors. She looked very proud, so even though I didn't approve of what was going to happen to her prisoners, I said, "Wow, I'm impressed," or something stupid like that.

"They'll have to boil for a long time before we can sink our teeth into them," she said, a cold-blooded killer look in her eye, "but then we'll have a banquet, right here on the beach."

"I can't wait," I said, moving toward the nearest palm tree. The trees grow right next to the water here. It looked wild, like it must have when Columbus dropped in. If you didn't look at the pink house, you could imagine yourself on a deserted tropical island. I lay down on one of the big towels she had spread out, and soon she came over and sat down real close to me. She got her thermos out of a sack and two plastic cups. She poured us some café con leche, which I usually hate because it's like ultra-sweet milk with a little coffee added for color or something. Nobody here asks you if you want cream or sugar in your coffee: the coffee *is* 99 percent cream and sugar. Take it or leave it. But at that hour on that beach, it tasted just right.

"Where is Papá?" I was getting curious about what he was doing in the pink house, and about who lived there.

"He is having a session with the *señora* and her daughter. That poor niña is not doing very well. Pobrecita. Poor little thing. I saw her when I helped him bring his things in this morning. She is a skeleton. Only sixteen, and she has packed her bags for the other world."

"She's that sick? Maybe they ought to take her to the hospital."

"How is your asthma, *mi amor?*" she said, apparently reminded of my own serious illness.

"Great. My asthma is great." I poured myself another cup of coffee. "So why don't they get a doctor for this girl?" I was getting pretty good at keeping conversations more or less on track with at least one person. "What exactly are her symptoms?"

"There was a man there," she said, totally ignoring my question, "not her *papá*, a man with a look that said *mala influencia* all over it." She shook her head and made a *tsk, tsk* sound. This real-life telenovela was beginning to get interesting.

"You mean he's a bad influence on the girl?"

"It is hard to explain, hija. A mala influencia is something that some people who are sensitive to spiritual matters can feel when they go into a house. Juan and I both felt chilled in there." She nodded toward the pink house.

"Maybe they have air conditioning," I said.

"And the feeling of evil got stronger when *ese hombre*, that strange man, came into the room," she added.

"Who is he?"

"The mother's boyfriend."

"So what's going to happen now?"

"It depends on what Juan decides is wrong with this *casa*. The mother is not very stable. She has money from a former husband, so it is not from physical need that these women suffer. La señora is fortunately a believer, and that is good for her daughter."

"Why?"

"Because she may do what needs to be done, if not for herself, then for her child—when a mala influencia takes over a house, *pues*, it affects everyone in it."

"Tell me some things that may happen, Mamá."

It was so strange that this rich woman had asked my grandfather to come solve her problems. I mean if things were going this crazy-wrong, someone should call a shrink, right? Here they got the local medicine man to make a house call.

"Well, Juan will interview each of the people under the mala influencia. Separately. So they don't get their stories tangled up, sabes? Then he will decide which spirits need to be contacted for help."

"Oh," I said, like it all sounded logical to me. Actually, I thought all Mamá had said was not too exciting for a supernatural event. Until she got to the part about contacting the spirits, that is.

"In most of these cases where a restless or bad spirit has settled over a house, it's just a matter of figuring out what it wants or needs. Then you have to help it to find its way to God by giving it a way out—giving it light. The home is purified of the bad influence, and peace returns."

We had a few minutes of quiet then, since she apparently thought she had made it all crystal clear to me, and I was trying to absorb some of the mumbo-jumbo I had just heard. But I got distracted looking at how the sunlight was sparkling off the water. I was feeling pretty good. Must be the caffeine kicking in, I thought.

"*Ven*"—my grandmother pulled me up by the hand; for a pudgy old lady she was pretty strong—"we have to bring dinner in."

So for a while we dragged the crab traps out. She wouldn't let me touch the crabs, since I didn't know how to handle them. "Might bite your fingers off," she explained calmly. So I went for a long walk down the beach. It turned out to be part of an inlet, which was why the water was so still, almost no waves. And I actually found some shells. This was new to me, since the public beach my cousins and I went to was swept clean of trash and everything else, every morning. Sand was all that was left until it was covered by empty cans, bags, disposable diapers, and all the other things people bring for a day at the beach and leave behind as a little gift to Mother Nature. But this was different. How could that girl in the pink house be so unhappy when she could wake up to this every morning?

I sat down on a sea-washed rock that was so smooth and comfortable I could just lounge on it all day. I stared out as far as I could see, and I thought I saw something jump out of the water. Not just one, but two or three—dolphins! Just like at Sea World. They jumped out, made a sort of half circle in the air, then went back under. I couldn't believe it. I ran back to my grandmother, who was stirring a big black pot over a fire, looking like the witch cooking something tasty for Hansel and Gretel. Gasping for air, which made her frown—that old asthma again—I told her what I had seen. I didn't know the Spanish word for dolphin, so I said "Flipper."

"Ah, sí, Fleeperr," she said, rolling that r forever like they do here, "*delfines*." She knew what I was talking about. "They like these waters, no fishermen, except for me, ha, ha." I avoided looking into the pot—strange sounds were coming from it.

"Wow," I said to myself. Dolphins. I couldn't wait to tell Meli. I had seen real wild dolphins.

Mamá Ana handed me a sandwich, and after I ate it, I fell asleep on the towel. I woke up when I heard Papá Juan's voice. I pretended to be still sleeping so I could listen in on an uncensored version of the weird stuff happening in the pink house. Mamá Ana had made a tent over our spot on the beach with four sticks and a blanket. She was working over the campfire, pouring things into the pot. I was getting hungry. Whatever she was cooking smelled great. Papá Juan was writing things in a notebook with a pencil that he kept wetting by putting it into his mouth. I was watching them from the corner of my eyes, not moving. It was Mamá who spoke first.

"It's that man, verdad?" She spoke very softly. I guess she didn't want to wake me up. I had to really strain to hear.

"I have told the mother that her house needs a spiritual cleansing. The mala influencia has settled over the young girl, but the evil has spread over everything. It is a very cold house."

"I felt it too," Mamá said, making the sign of the cross over her face and chest.

"It is the man who is the agent. He has brought bad ways with him. He has frightened the girl. She will not tell me how."

"I saw a bruise on her arm."

"Sí." My grandfather put his notebook down and seemed to go into a trance or something. He closed his eyes and let his head drop. His lips were moving. I watched Mamá to see what she would do, but she continued cooking like nothing unusual was happening. Then he sort of shook his head like he was just trying to wake up, and went back to writing in his notebook.

"Have you decided what to do?" Mamá came to sit next to him and peeked over his shoulder at the notebook. She nodded, agreeing with whatever it was.

"I will tell the mother that she must not allow this man into the house anymore. Then I will prepare the herbs for her so that next Tuesday and Friday she can clean the house and fumigate."

"What about the niña?" Mamá asked. They had their heads together like two doctors discussing a patient.

"I will treat her with some of our comadre's tea. I will also tell her that the only way for us to get rid of the evil in the house is with her help. She will have to work with her mother."

"The woman will not want to throw the man out."

"You will have to help me convince her of the consequences if she doesn't, Ana. She is a believer. And although she is misguided, she loves her daughter."

"We have to bring light into this home, Juan."

"The girl saw Rita from her window. She asked who

she was," my grandfather said. "Let us send our niña to invite Angela for dinner."

"Good idea," said Mamá.

Great, I thought, great idea. Send me over to get the girl from *The Exorcist*—good way to ruin my day at the beach.

"Rita! Hija!" Mamá called out loudly. "Time to wake up!"

The house was pale pink on the inside too. The woman who answered my knock was a surprise. She looked elegant in a white sundress. She also looked familiar to me. I guess I must have stared because she said, "I'm Maribel Hernández Jones," like I should recognize the name. Seeing that I didn't, she added, "You may know me from TV. I do toothpaste commercials." That was it. Her commercial had come on about five times during the telenovela.

"I'm Rita. My grandmother wants to know if Angela would like to eat with us." The smile faded into a sad look, but she pointed to a closed door at the other end of the room. The place was like a dollhouse. All the furniture was white and looked like no one ever sat on it.

The girl must have heard me or else been spying from her window, because I'd barely gotten to her door when she flew out, grabbing my hand. We were out of the house before I ever got a good look at her. Shorter than I was by about four inches, she was very thin. She had long black hair and beautiful, sort of bronze skin. Still, she looked kind of pale too, like you do when you've been sick for a while.

"I'm sorry," she said in English, which surprised me, "I just had to get out of there. I'm Angela." We shook hands.

"You speak English," I said, noticing the huge ring on her thin finger. She was also wearing a gold bracelet. This was a rich girl.

"My stepfather was an American," she said. "We spent a lot of time with him in New York before he died."

"Oh," I said, thinking, I see where the money came from now.

My grandmother had already set out plates and bowls for the crab stew she had made. I ate like a fiend. I was starved. The beach always makes me extra hungry, even when I don't swim. Angela ate a few spoonfuls and put the bowl down. My grandmother put the bowl back in her hands. "I spent all day catching the crabs and cooking them, *señorita*. Do me the honor of eating a little more." She was outrageous. She actually watched Angela as the poor kid forced it all down—you could tell it was an effort. Here is the secret weapon against anorexia, I thought: my grandmother.

It wasn't long before the mother came out to get her daughter. "We have to talk," she said. Mamá and Papá nodded. It was part of the plan, I could see that. I was a little disappointed; I had really been looking forward to getting a little more information directly from the source. Angela looked at me as if she wanted to stay longer too. Then Mamá Ana spoke up.

"In two weeks we are having a *quinceañera* party for Rita. I would like Angela to come."

Angela smiled and kissed her on both cheeks. Mamá hugged her like she did me, that is, so hard that you can't breathe. It didn't seem to take long for people to get familiar with each other around here.

I had thought that the party had just been something

Mamá had made up at the beach, but it turned out that she meant it. Although the next two weeks were mainly the usual routines of eating too much, drinking café, watching telenovelas, and accompanying Papá to two more jobs— neither one as interesting as Angela's case: one turned out to be a simple problem of envy between two sisters, easily handled with special charms Papá carved for them himself; and the other was a cheating husband who was told that he would be haunted forever by the restless spirit of a man shot by his wife if he did not give up womanizing—Mamá and I spent some time shopping for my dress, with money Mamá had had my mother send us, and for food and dec- orations for the house. It all seemed pretty childish, but on the island they make a big deal of a girl's turning fifteen. I wondered who she was going to invite besides Angela, since I didn't know anyone except old relatives like her. No problem, parties are for everybody, she explained, old relatives, neighbors, kids. Apparently, I was just the excuse to have a blowout.

I chose a blue satin cocktail dress my mother would never have let me buy. Mamá thought it was *muy bonito*, very pretty, even if we had to stuff a little toilet paper in the bra to fill out the bodice.

The party started at noon on a Saturday. There was a ton of food set out on tables in the backyard under a mango tree, and there were Japanese lanterns hanging from the branches, which we would light when it got dark, and a portable record player—about fifty years old—ready to blast out salsa music. I had a few of my tapes of *good* music with me for my Walkman, but there was no player or stereo anywhere around. People piled into the house and hugged and kissed me. I was starting to get a headache when a long white limousine pulled up to the front of our house. Angela and her mother stepped out of it. I looked to see if the "mala influencia" man was with them, but the car drove away. A chauffeur too. Wow. Everyone had stopped talking when Mamá's big-mouthed neighbor shouted, "Oh, my God, it's Maribel Hernández!" And people crowded around her before she could step inside. I saw Angela trying politely to come through several large sweaty women, and I reached for her hand and led her to my room. I had to shoo Ramón off my bed, where he was getting ready to crow, before we sat down. Angela laughed at the crazy rooster, and I saw that she looked different. She didn't have that pale greenish color under her skin. She was still skinny, but she looked healthier.

She winked at me and said, "It worked."

"What worked?" I had no idea what she was talking about.

Outside my door the noise level was climbing. People were pouring out into the yard, which was right outside my window. I saw Mamá Ana dancing up a storm in the middle of a circle of people. When she had taken her bows, she started making her way through the crowd of short people like a small tank aiming right for my room. Papá Juan was taking Ramón around, apparently introducing him to the guests, or trying to keep him from getting trampled to death. I had to give him credit; he didn't seem to care if he made a fool of himself. But most people in town seemed to think he was pretty great. I watched him looking at each guest with his kind brown eyes, and I asked myself whether he really could see inside their heads and their hearts.

"Your grandfather's cure. *Mami* and I cleaned our house from top to bottom. No more bad influences left in it; the first thing we've done together in months. And best of all, she threw him out."

"Rita, Rita!" It was my grandmother, yelling out for me over the noise of people, scratchy records, and a hysterical rooster. "It's time to sing 'Feliz Cumpleaños'!" She looked great in her bright red party dress and seemed to be having a blast. She had this talent for turning every day into a sort of party. I had to laugh.

"I can't believe this," I said to Angela, falling back on the bed and putting my face under a pillow. She giggled and pulled the pillow away from me.

"You'll get used to it," she said. "I wish I had a grandmother like yours. Both of mine are dead."

"You can borrow mine," I offered.

"Come on," she said, and we both jumped off the bed, with me nearly breaking my neck on my new high heels.

The party was fun with Angela there. Even her mother seemed to be enjoying herself, although people continuously bugged her for autographs. I even saw somebody handing her a magazine with a toothpaste ad for her to sign. She just kept smiling and smiling.

They stayed until after midnight, when the last person went home. Papá was snoring in his rocking chair, and Mamá and Angela's mother were cleaning the kitchen. Angela and I talked in my room. We agreed to get together as much as possible until I had to go back home to Paterson. Even then, she said, she would come visit me. She had money to travel.

I spent a lot of time at the pink house over the next weeks. I even began liking the color. I told Angela about

Johnny Ruiz even though I had not really thought about him, not as much anyway, in the last month. She said that he sounded like a troubled boy. A mala influencia? I suggested. We both laughed at the thought of Johnny's being followed around by a restless ghost. The whole thing with him and Joey Molieri, and the mess with Meli's and my parents, began to seem like a movie I had seen a long time ago. And one day, while we were walking down the beach after dinner, she told me about how hard her life had been, moving from place to place while her mother was trying to make it on TV. She had spent a lot of time with babysitters, especially after her father had left them, when Angela was just five.

"Where is he now?" I asked her.

"He lives in New York with his new family. I plan to go see him when I visit you. My mother only lets him come down once a year. But we've been talking about it, and she thinks I can take care of myself now. See, he's not a bad man, but sometimes he drinks too much. That's what started the trouble between them."

Then she told me about Mr. Jones, a rich guy who owned hotels. He had left them the pink house and a lot of money when he died in a small-plane crash a year ago. Angela said that he had been a nice guy too, although not too interested in her, or in much else besides making money. But the man whom she really hated was the boyfriend who had recently been chased out by an "evil spirit." Angela laughed when she said that, but got serious when she told me it had been a really awful time. That's when her mother had called in Don Juan, as she called Papá, for a consultation.

"Your mother seems like a smart person," I said. "Does

she really believe in all this ghost-evil spirit-haunted house stuff?"

"She's not the only one, Rita. Don't you see it took someone with special powers to drive out the bad influence in my house?" She looked at me in a really serious way for a minute; then she started giggling.

"Come on!" She started running back to the house. "It's time for the telenovela and my mother's new commercial!"

My family arrived in early August. We went to pick them up in three cars, with two more following for the welcoming committee. My mother kept looking at me at the airport. She acted like she was a little scared of coming too close. She had heard only from her mother about me—since I had forgotten to write home—and she must have thought Mamá Ana was probably exaggerating when she wrote that I was having a great time and had not had an asthma attack in weeks. They had never gotten it straight on the asthma, which my mother figured was one of my tricks. She knew me a little. Finally I gave her a break and came over and hugged her.

"You are so tanned, mi amor. Have you been to the beach a lot?"

I didn't want her to think it had all been a vacation, so I said, "A few times. Have you seen Meli?" She looked at me with a kind of sad look on her face, scaring me. I hadn't written to Meli either, so I didn't know whether she was dead, or what.

"You don't know? She went on that retreat with the sisters, you know. It turns out that she liked it. So she won't be at Central High with you next year. I'm sorry, hija. Meli is going to start school at St. Mary's in the fall."

I almost burst out laughing. Our parents had really come up with some awful punishments for Meli and me. I'd had one of the best summers of my life with Angela, and I was even really getting to know my grandparents—the Ghostbusting magnificent duo. I had been taking medium lessons from them lately, and had learned a few tricks, like how to look really closely at people and see whether something was bothering them. I saw in my mother's eyes that she was scared I might hate her for sending me away. And she should have been, so I let her suffer a little. But then I squeezed in next to her in Papá's toy car and held her hand while Mamá Ana told her all the intimate details about me, including the fact that she had cured my asthma with a special tea she had made me drink. I looked at my mother and winked. She gave me a loud kiss on my cheek that made my ears ring. I know now where she picked up that bad habit. Since I already knew everything Mamá Ana was going to tell my mother, being a mind reader myself now, I settled back to try to figure out how Meli and I were going to get together in September. I had heard St. Mary's basketball team had some of the best-looking guys.

Dawn

Tim Wynne-Jones

Barnsey met Dawn on the night bus to North Bay. His mother put him on at Ottawa, just after supper. His parents owned a store and the Christmas season was frantic, so for the third year in a row, Barnsey was going up to Grandma Barrymore's and his parents would follow Christmas day. He had cousins in North Bay, so it was fine with Barnsey, as long as he didn't have to sit beside someone weird the whole way.

"What if I have to sit beside someone weird the whole way?" he asked his mother in the bus terminal. She cast him a warning look. A let's-not-make-a-scene look. Barnsey figured she was in a hurry to get back to the store.

"You are thirteen, Matthew," she said. There was an edge in her voice that hadn't been there before. "Has anything bad happened to you yet?"

Barnsey was picking out a couple of magazines for the trip: *Guitar World* and *Sports Illustrated*. "I didn't say anything *bad* was going to happen. If anything *bad* happens, I make a racket and the bus driver deals with it. I know all that. I'm just talking about someone weird."

"For instance?" said his mother.

"Someone who smells. Someone really, really fat who spills over onto my seat. Someone who wants to talk about her liver operation."

His mother paid for the magazines and threw in a Kit Kat, too. Barnsey didn't remind her that she'd already bought him a Kit Kat, and let him buy a Coke, chips, and some gum. And this was apart from the healthy stuff she had already packed at home. She was usually pretty strict about junk food.

"I just asked," said Barnsey.

"Come on," said his mother, giving his shoulder a bit of a squeeze. "Or the only *weird* person you're going to be sitting beside is your mother on the way back to the store."

Barnsey didn't bother to ask if that was an option. His parents put a lot of stock in planning. They didn't put much stock in spontaneity.

"What if I end up in Thunder Bay by mistake?"

His mother put her arm around him. He was almost as tall as she was now. "Matthew," she said in her let's-be-rational voice. "That would require quite a mistake on your part. But, if it were to happen, you have a good head on your shoulders *and* your own bank card."

His mother almost looked as if she was going to say something about how they had always encouraged him to be independent, but luckily she noticed it was boarding time.

They were at Bay 6, and his mother suddenly gave him a very uncharacteristic hug. A bear hug. They weren't a hugging kind of family. She looked him in the eyes.

"Matthew," she said. "It's not so long. Remember that."

"I know," said Barnsey. But he wasn't sure if his mother meant the trip or the time before he'd see her again. He couldn't tell.

They moved through the line toward the driver, who was taking tickets at the door of the bus.

"Don't do the thing with the money," Barnsey whispered to his mother.

"Why not?" she said. Barnsey didn't answer. "It's just good business. And besides, young man, I'll do what I please."

And she did. As Barnsey gave the driver his ticket, Barnsey's mother ripped a twenty-dollar bill in half ceremoniously in front of the driver's face. She gave half the bill to Barnsey, who shoved it quickly in his pocket.

"Here, my good man," said his mother to the bus driver in her store voice. "My son will give you the other half upon arrival in North Bay. Merry Christmas."

The driver thanked her. But he gave Barnsey a secret kind of cockeyed look, as if to say, Does she pull this kind of stunt all the time?

Then Barnsey was on board the bus, and there was Dawn.

There was no other seat. His mother had once told him that if there weren't any seats left, the bus company would have to get a bus just for him. That was the way they did business. So Barnsey shuffled up and down the bus a couple of times even after he'd put his bag up top, looking—hoping—that someone would take the seat beside Dawn so he could triumphantly demand a bus of his own. But there were no other seats and no other passengers.

He suddenly wanted very much to go back out to his mother, even though she would say he was being irrational. But then when he caught a glimpse of her through the window, she looked almost as miserable as he felt. He remembered the bear hug with a shiver. It shook his resolve. Timidly he turned to Dawn.

"Is this seat taken?" he asked.

The girl took off her Walkman earphones and stared at the seat a bit, as if looking for someone. She took a long time.

"Doesn't look like it."

Barnsey sat down and made himself comfortable. He got out his own Walkman and arranged his tapes on his lap and thought about the order in which he was going to eat all the junk he had or whether he'd eat a bit of each thing—the chocolate bars, the chips, the Coke—in some kind of order so they all came out even. At home his mother had packed a loganberry soda and some trail mix. He'd keep those for last. Strictly emergency stuff.

Then the bus driver came on board and they were off.

"There's talk of big snow up the valley a way, so I'm gonna light a nice cozy fire," he said. People chuckled. There was already a cozy kind of nighttime we're-stuck-in-this-together mood on the bus. Nobody was drunk or too loud. And the girl beside Barnsey seemed to be completely engrossed in whatever was coming through her earphones.

It was only the way she looked that he had any problem with. The nine earrings, the nose rings, and the Mohawk in particular—orange along the scalp and purple along the crest as if her skull was a planet and the sun was coming up on the horizon of her head. She was about twenty and dressed all in black, with clunky black Doc Martens. But as long as she was just going to listen to her music, then Barnsey would listen to his and everything would be fine.

And it was for the first hour or so. By then the bus had truly slipped into a comfortable humming silence. It was about nine, and some people were sleeping. Others were talking softly as if they didn't want to wake a baby in the next room. That's when the mix-up occurred.

There isn't much room in a bus seat. And there wasn't much room on Barnsey's lap. Somehow a couple of his tapes slid off him into the space between him and Dawn, the girl with the horizon on her head, though he didn't know her name yet. The weird thing was, the same thing had happened to her tapes. And the weirdest thing of all was that they both found out at just about the same time.

Barnsey shoved the new Xiphoid Process tape into his machine and punched it on. While he was waiting for the music to start, he dug the cassette out from his backpack and looked again at the hologram cover. The band was standing under lowering skies all around an eerie-looking gravestone. Then if you tipped the cover just right, the guys all seemed to pull back, and there was a hideous ghoul all covered with dirt and worms standing right in the middle of them where the grave marker had been. It was great.

Barnsey pulled a bag of chips from the backpack at his feet, squeezed it so that the pressure in the bag made it pop open, and crunched on a couple of chips as quietly as he could. He was busy enjoying the way the first sour cream and onion chip tastes, and it took him a minute to notice he wasn't hearing anything.

He turned the volume up a bit. Nothing. Then he realized there *was* something. A tinkling noise and a bit of a whooshing noise, and a bit of what sounded like rain and some dripping and more tinkling.

Barnsey banged his Walkman. He thought the batteries were dying. Then Dawn changed tapes as well and suddenly yelled, as if she'd just touched a hot frying pan. Some people looked around angrily. The looks on their faces made Barnsey think they had just been waiting for a chance to glare at her. One lady glanced at him, too, in a pitying kind of way, as if to say, Poor young thing. Having to sit beside a banshee like that.

Meanwhile, both of them opened up their Walkmans like Christmas presents. They held their tapes up to the little lights above them to check the titles.

"Rain Forest with Temple Bells?" Barnsey read out loud.

"'Scream for Your Supper!'" Dawn read out loud.

Barnsey apologized, nervously. Dawn just laughed. They made the switch, but before Barnsey could even say thank you, the girl suddenly took his tape back.

"Tell you what," she said. "You listen to that fer 'alf a mo, and I'll give this a try. 'kay?"

She had a thick accent, British.

"Okay," said Barnsey, "but I think yours is broken or something."

She took her tape back and tried it. She smiled, and her smile was good. It kind of stretched across her face and curled up at the ends.

"Naa," she said. "Ya just 'av ta listen, mate. Closely, like."

So Barnsey listened closely. He turned it up. There was a rain forest. There were ravens croaking and other birds twittering away. And there were bells. He thought someone was playing them, but after a while he realized that it was just the rain playing them, the wind. He kept waiting for the music to start. He didn't know what the music would be. Any moment a drum would kick in, he thought, then a synthesizer all warbly and a guitar keening high and distorted and a thumping bass and, last of all, a voice. Maybe singing about trees. About saving them.

But no drum kicked in. Maybe the tape *was* broken?

It took him a minute to realize Dawn was tapping him on the shoulder. She had his Xiphoid Process tape in her hand and a cranky look on her face.

"This is killer-diller," she said.

"You like X.P.?" he asked.

"It's rubbish."

Barnsey laughed. *Rubbish*. What a great word. He pulled out Rain Forest with Temple Bells.

"What ya think?" she asked.

"It's rubbish."

Then they both started to giggle. And now people stared at them as if they were in cahoots and going to ruin the whole trip for everyone. Dawn hit him on the arm to shush him up.

He showed her the hologram cover of the X.P. tape.

"You think it's their mum?" she asked.

"Maybe," he said. He wished he could think of something to say. He just flipped the picture a few times. She leaned toward him. Her hand out.

"Dawn," she whispered.

It took him a minute to realize she was introducing herself. "Barnsey," he whispered back, as if it was a code. He shook her hand.

He offered her some chips. She took the whole bag and made a big deal of holding it up to the light so she could read the ingredients. She shuddered.

"It's a bleedin' chemical plant in 'ere," she said.

"Rubbish," said Barnsey. Then he dug out the trail mix

and they both settled down to listen to their own tapes. Barnsey turned X.P. down to 2 because there was no way Dawn would be able to hear her forest with Spice-box wailing on the guitar and Mickey Slick pounding on the drums. After a couple of cuts he switched it off altogether.

He found himself thinking of the time he had traveled with his father out to British Columbia, where he was from, to Denman Island. He remembered the forest there, like nothing he'd ever seen in southern Ontario. Vast and high. It had been a lovely summer day with the light sifting down through the trees. But, he thought, if it rained there, it would sound like Dawn's tape.

He didn't put a tape in his cassette. He left the earphones on and listened to the hum of the bus instead.

"It's not so long."

It was the bus driver. Barnsey woke up with his mouth feeling like the inside of a bread box.

There was a stirring all around. People waking, stretching, chattering sleepily and my-my-ing as they looked out the windows. The bus was stopped.

"Will ya lookit that," said Dawn. Her nose was pressed up against the window. Outside was a nothingness of white.

They had pulled off the highway into a football field–sized parking lot. Another bus was parked up ahead. Through the swirling blizzard they could see lots of trucks and cars in the lot. It wasn't the stop Barnsey remembered from previous trips.

Barnsey could see the driver standing outside without his jacket, his shoulders hunched against the driving snow. He was talking to another bus driver, nodding his head a lot and stamping his feet to keep warm. Then he hopped back on the bus and closed the door behind him.

"Seems like we've got ourselves a little unscheduled stop," he said. "The road's bunged up clear through to Mattawa."

Someone asked him a question. Somebody interrupted with another question. The driver did a lot of answering and nodding and shaking his head and reassuring. Barnsey just looked over Dawn's shoulder at the outside, shivering a bit from sleepiness and the sight of all that whirling snow. Dawn smelled nice. Not exotic like the perfume his mother wore, but kind of bracing and clean.

"This here place doesn't have a name," said the driver. People laughed. He was making it all sound like fun. "But the barn there with all the blinking lights is called the Cattle Yard, and the owner says yer'all welcome to come on down and warm yerself up a spell."

Passengers immediately started to get up and stretch and fish around for handbags and sweaters and things. There was an air of excitement on the bus. The Cattle Yard was a big roadhouse painted fire-engine red and lit up with spotlights. It was no ordinary way station.

Still sleepy, Barnsey made no effort to move as people started to file past him pulling on their coats. Dawn still had her nose pressed up against the glass.

"D'ya know where I spent last Christmas?" she said. Barnsey thought for a moment, as if maybe she'd told him and he'd forgotten.

"In Bethlehem," she said.

"*The* Bethlehem?"

"That's right," she said. "In a bar."

Barnsey looked at Dawn. She was smiling but not like she was fooling. "There are bars in Bethlehem?"

She laughed. "Brilliant bars. Smashing litt'l town is Bethlehem."

Barnsey tried to imagine it.

Then the bus driver was beside him. "Here, you might need this," he said. And with a flick of his fingers he produced the half-a-twenty Barnsey's mother had given him. Barnsey was about to explain that it was meant to be a tip, but the driver waved his hand in protest. "Just don't get yourself all liquored up, son," he said, and then, laughing and clapping Barnsey on the back, he headed out of the bus.

"Wha's that then?" asked Dawn, looking at the half-a-twenty-dollar bill. Barnsey pulled the other half out of his pants pocket and held them side by side.

"Hungry?" he said.

And she was hungry. He hadn't realized how skinny she was, but she stored away a grilled cheese sandwich in no time and two pieces of apple pie with ice cream. She ordered hot water and fished a tea bag from deep in her ratty black leather jacket.

"Ginseng, mate," she said. "Nothing illegal."

But Barnsey had only been noticing how stained the tea bag was and the little tab at the end of the string which had strange characters written on it.

It was all so strange. Strange for Barnsey to walk into a place with her, as if they were on a date—a thirteen-year-old and a twenty-year-old. He wondered if people thought she was his sister. He couldn't imagine his parents putting up with the way Dawn looked. She sure turned heads at the Cattle Yard. He wasn't sure if he minded or not. In his burgundy L. L. Bean coat, he didn't exactly look like he belonged in the place, either.

It was a huge smoke-filled bar with moose antlers on the knotty pine walls and two or three big TVs around the room tuned into the Nashville Network. There was a Leafs game on the TV over the bar. Just about everyone was wearing a trucker's hat, and nobody looked like they were leaving until maybe Christmas.

The bus passengers were herded down to one end where a section had been closed off but was now reopened. The bus drivers smoked and made phone calls and made jokes to their passengers about not getting on the wrong bus when they left and ending up in Timbuktu. Through the window and the blizzard of snow, Barnsey watched another bus roll in.

"I saw three ships cum sailin' in," sang Dawn. She was picking at Barnsey's leftover french fries—*chips*, she called them—trying to find ones that didn't have any burger juice on them. She was a vegetarian.

"Bloody heathen," she'd called him when he'd ordered a bacon burger and fries. He loved that.

"I've gotta go find the loo," she said.

"Bloody heathen," he said.

She flicked him on the nose with a chip as she clomped by in her Doc Martens. He wondered if it was possible to walk quietly in them.

"Rubbish," he said. He watched her walk through the bar toward the washrooms. Somebody must have said something to her because she suddenly stopped and turned back to a table where five guys in trucking caps were sitting. They looked like all together they probably weighed a ton, but that didn't seem to bother Dawn. She leaned up close to one of them, her fists curled menacingly, and snarled something right at his face.

Barnsey watched in horror, imagining a scene from some movie where the whole place would erupt into a beer-slinging, window-smashing brawl. Instead, the guy whose face she was talking at suddenly roared with laughter and slapped the tabletop. The other four guys laughed, too. One of them ended up spitting half a mug of beer all over his friends. Then Dawn shook hands with her tormentors and sauntered off to the loo, as she called it.

Barnsey felt like he would burst with admiration. He picked up her teacup and smelled the ginseng. It smelled deadly. The writing on the little tab was Indian, he guessed. From India.

He looked around. On the big TV a country song-stress with big country hair and dressed in a beautiful country-blue dress was draping silver tinsel on a Christmas tree while she sang about somebody being home for Christmas. Then the image would cut to that somebody in a half-ton truck fighting his way through a blizzard. Same boat we're in, thought Barnsey. Then the image would cut back to the Christmas tree and then to a flashback of the couple walking up a country road with a bouncy dog, having an argument in the rain and so on. Then back to the guy in the truck, the girl by the tree. It was a whole little minimovie.

Barnsey found himself trying to imagine X.P. dressing that same tinselly Christmas tree in that nice living room. But of course the guy in the truck trying to get home for Christmas would be the grim reaper or something, with worms crawling out of its eyes.

Then Dawn came back.

"What did you say to that guy?" Barnsey asked.

She smiled mysteriously. "I told 'im that if 'e'd said what 'e said to me in Afghanistan, 'e'd'ave to marry me on the spot."

It was around eleven before word came through that it was safe to leave. The drivers got everybody sorted out and back on board. Everyone at the Cattle Yard yelled Merry Christmas and held up their beer glasses in a toast. The guy who had been rude to Dawn stood and bowed as she passed by, and she curtsied. Then she made as if she was going to bite off his nose, which made his ton of friends roar again, their fat guts shaking with laughter.

By then Barnsey knew that Dawn had just got back from Nepal, where she'd been traveling with "'er mate" ever since she left Israel, where she'd been working on a kibbutz after arriving there from Bloody Cairo, where she'd had all her kit stolen. Before that she'd been in Ghana and before that art school. Barnsey didn't know what a kit was, or a kibbutz. He wasn't sure where Nepal was, either, or what or who 'er mate might be. But he didn't ask. She'd called him mate, too.

On the bus the excitement of the unscheduled stop soon died down. The roads were only passable so it was slow going. It was kind of nice that the three buses were traveling together. In a convoy, the driver had called it. It sounded reassuring. Soon people were falling asleep, snoring. But not Barnsey. He sat thinking. Trying to imagine working on a flower farm in Israel, the heat, the fragrance of it. Trying to imagine Bethlehem.

"Was it cold?"

"Freezin' at night," she said.

"See any stables?"

She laughed. "No, but I did see a good-sized shed behind a McDonald's."

Barnsey laughed. He tried to imagine the holy family pulling into Bethlehem today and huddling down in a shed out back of a McDonald's. Maybe Joseph would have a Big Mac. But Mary? Probably a vegetarian, he decided.

Quietness again.

"What kind of a store is it your people 'ave, master Barnsey?"

"A gift store," he said.

"Ah, well," said Dawn. "I can imagine a gift store would be busy at Christmas."

Finally, Barnsey dozed off. And the next thing he knew, the bus was slowing down and driving through the deserted streets of North Bay. It was past 2:00 A.M.

"That'll be 'er," said Dawn as they pulled into the bus terminal. Somehow she had recognized his grandma Barrymore in the little knot of worried folks waiting.

Barnsey just sat drowsily for a minute while people stirred around him. He felt like he weighed a ton.

"Get on with ya," said Dawn in a cheery voice. And she made a big joke of shoving him and roughhousing him out of his seat as if he was Dumbo the elephant. Then she gathered up all his wrappers and cans and threw them at him, saying, "'Ere—lookit this! Yer not leavin' this for me, I'ope." Barnsey found himself, weak with laughter, herded down the aisle. At the door he said good-bye and hoped that her trip to Vancouver would be nothing but rubbish the whole way. Grandma Barrymore was standing at the foot of the bus stairs. Much to her surprise, Dawn grabbed Barnsey by the head and scrubbed it hard with her knuckle.

"In Afghanistan, you'd have to marry me for that," said Barnsey.

"Toodle-oo, mate," said Dawn, blowing him a kiss. She blew one at Grandma Barrymore, too.

Dawn would arrive in Vancouver on Christmas Eve. Barnsey thought of her often over the next couple of days. He'd check his watch and imagine her arriving in Winnipeg, although all he knew of Winnipeg was the Blue Bombers football stadium which he'd seen on TV. And then Regina and Calgary. He imagined the three buses like wise men still traveling across the country in a convoy. But as much as Barnsey thought about Dawn, he gave up trying to talk to anyone about her. Grandma had seen her but only long enough to get the wrong impression. And when Barnsey tried to tell his cousins about her, it came out like a cartoon, with her wacky hair and her fat black boots. He couldn't get Dawn across to them—the *life of* her—only the image of her, so he stopped trying.

There was a lot to do, anyway. His cousins had arranged a skating party and Grandma wanted him to go shopping with her and help with some chores around the house. He enjoyed all the attention she showered on him. She spoiled him rotten just the way she'd spoiled his father rotten, she liked to say. But he'd never noticed it quite so much as this year. Anything he looked at, she asked him if he wanted it. It was spooky.

Then it was Christmas morning. It was a four-hour drive from Ottawa. His parents would arrive by 1:00 P.M. and that's when the celebration would start. When he saw his father's Mustang coming up the driveway at 10:30 A.M., Barnsey knew something was wrong.

He didn't go to the door. He watched from the window. They should have come in the big car. But there wasn't any they. Just his dad.

"Matthew, go help your dad with his parcels," said Grandma.

"No," said Barnsey. He was remembering the last time he had looked at his mother in the bus terminal, through the window. The look on her face. "It won't be so long," she had said.

It wasn't that his mother was sick or there was some problem at the store; they would have phoned. Barnsey's mind grew icy sharp. Everything was suddenly clear to him. He could see a trail of incidents leading to this if he thought about it. You just had to tilt life a bit, and there was a whole other picture.

His parents weren't very talkative. They didn't chatter; they didn't argue. And yet in the moments while his father unpacked the trunk of his salt-stained Mustang and made his way back and forth up the path Barnsey had shoveled so clean just the night before, Barnsey could hear in his head all the signs and hints stretching back through the months—how far, he wasn't sure. Right up to now, the past few days, with Grandma so attentive. Spoiling him rotten.

Then his father was in the living room, still in his coat, waiting for Barnsey to say something. His face didn't look good but to Barnsey he didn't look anywhere near bad enough, all things considered. Grandma Barrymore was standing behind him with her hand on her son's shoulder. She looked very sad. They waited. Barnsey looked out the window. Old-fashioned lace curtains hung across the living-room window. They were always there, even when the drapes were open. Barnsey stood between the lace and the cold glass. He turned and looked at his grandma through the veil of the curtain.

"I wish you'd told me," he said.

"She didn't know, Matthew," said his father. "Not for sure."

The ball was back in his court. That was the way his parents were with him. Lots of room. His father would not press him. He could wait forever and his father would never start saying stuff like "I'm sorry, honey," or "It's all for the better," or "Your mother still loves you, Matthew." Barnsey could wait forever and he wouldn't see his father cry. He would have done his crying already, if he had any crying to do. His parents didn't hold much with spontaneity.

He glanced at his father in his black coat and white silk scarf. He wanted him to do something.

Barnsey stared out the window.

"When did you get the ski rack," he said.

"When I needed something to carry skis."

There was a pair of skis on the top of the car. Rossignols.

"They're yours," said his father. "I couldn't exactly wrap them."

Barnsey had been wanting downhill skis. And one of the large boxes piled in the hall was probably a good pair of ski boots. His parents would have read consumer reports about this. Even while they were breaking up.

"Your mother is hoping maybe you'll go on a skiing trip with her later in the holidays. Maybe Vermont."

"That would be nice," said Barnsey. Then he left the window and went to his room. His father didn't follow. It was his way of showing respect. He didn't say that; he didn't have to. He was there for him. He didn't say that, either, but it was something Barnsey had heard often. "We're here for you, chum."

Barnsey stayed in his room a long time, long enough to hear both sides of the new X.P. tape he hadn't had time to listen to on the bus. He flipped the cassette cover again and again. The ghoul glowed and vanished. Glowed and vanished.

Then his mother phoned. They had probably worked all this out, too.

"Must have been a terrible shock . . .

"Decided it was best this way . . .

"We couldn't dissolve the partnership in time for the shopping season. . . .

"Couldn't see us play-acting our way through Christmas . . ."

Barnsey listened. Said the right things.

"Do you think we could head down to Mount Washington for a long weekend?" said his mother. "Give those new skis a workout?"

"They aren't new," said Barnsey.

"They sure are," said his mother. "They're the best."

"There's a lot of snow between here and Ottawa," said Barnsey. It took his mother a minute to realize it was a joke. A lame kind of joke.

Then, with plans tentatively set and the call over and his mother's voice gone, Barnsey joined his father and his father's mother in the living room. They both gave him hugs.

"You okay?" his father asked.

"Yes."

"You want to talk now? Or later?"

"Later," he said.

"I think we all need a sherry," said Grandma. She poured Barnsey a glass. He liked the idea better than the sherry.

They ate lunch and then, since it was Christmas, they sat in the living room opening presents. Barnsey kept glancing at his father, expecting to see a little telltale tear or something. But all he ever glimpsed were the concerned looks his father was giving him.

He took his father's place as the hander-outer. When he came to his own present for his mother, he said, "Where should I put this?" His father piled the package on a chair in the hall.

Barnsey wasn't looking forward to Christmas dinner at his aunt's. His father had already taken that into consideration and would stay with him at Grandma's, if he liked. They'd make something special, just the two of them. But when he phoned to explain things, his sister wouldn't hear of them not coming, and his cousins got on the phone and begged Barnsey to come and try out their new computer game and in the end he went. Nobody talked about his mother not being there, at least not while Barnsey was around. Everyone was really considerate.

In bed he lay thinking about what kind of a place his mother would live in. She was the one leaving the relationship, so she was the one leaving the house. Barnsey wondered whether there would be a room for him or whether she'd just make up a couch when he came to visit. Then he wondered if his father would stay in Ottawa or move back to the west coast. He lay trying to think of as many things as could possibly go wrong so that he wouldn't be surprised by anything.

"I just wish someone had told me," he said.

"We'll turn it around, Matthew," his father had said

when he came to say good-night. "We'll make this into a beginning."

Was that from some kind of a book? How could he say that? Couldn't he tell the difference between a beginning and an ending?

There wasn't another man in his mother's life. His father hadn't found another woman.

"At least it isn't messy," his father said. He needn't have bothered. Nothing they ever did was messy.

In his sleep, Barnsey escaped. He found himself back on the bus.

"Rubbish," Dawn kept saying, and she pounded her fist into her palm every time she said it. Then the man in the seat ahead of them turned around, and it was the guy who had been in the country video heading home in his half-ton through a blizzard to his tinsel-happy lady.

"Rubbish," he said. And then all of Xiphoid Process, who were *also* on the bus, turned around in their seats, pounding their fists and saying, "Rubbish. Rubbish. Rubbish." Soon the bus driver joined in and the whole bus sang a "Hallelujah Chorus" of "Rubbish, rubbish, rubbish."

Barnsey woke up, his head spinning. All he could think about was rubbish. He thought about the talk he had to have with his father that day. His father wouldn't insist, but he would be expecting it. He would say all the right things and, before Barnsey knew it, *he* would be saying all the right things, too. They'd talk it out. Get things out in the open. It would all make perfect sense.

Rubbish.

So he left.

He didn't pack a bag, only stuffed a couple of extra things in his backpack. He wasn't sure what a ticket to

Vancouver cost, but it didn't matter. He had his bank card. He had no idea what he was going to do and he didn't care. He would not run away like his mother, carefully planning it all out first. How far did that get you?

And so, by nine o'clock on Boxing Day morning, he was at the bus terminal, a ticket in his pocket, sitting, waiting. He had his Walkman with him and he rooted around in his backpack for a tape other than X.P. He didn't think he could take that right now.

He had five or six tapes in the bottom of his bag. He hadn't emptied it since the trip. He pulled them out one by one: Alice in Chains, Guns 'n' Roses, Nirvana, Rain Forest with Temple Bells—

Rain Forest with Temple Bells?

Barnsey stared at the tape. He must have packed it up in the dark of the bus without noticing. Then he saw a piece of paper sticking out of the edge of the cassette. He opened the cassette and took out a folded-up note written in pencil.

> dear barnsey this is for the meal and for the fun
> and for when the rubbish gets to be too much but
> you're snoring while i write this so maybe i'll
> shove the note in your gob!!! no i won't i'll hide it
> and it'll be your xmas present from dawn xox

Barnsey found himself shaking. He read the note again and again. He smelled it—trying to catch her scent—and held it and then folded it up carefully and put it back in the cassette. He took out the tape and put it on. He closed his eyes and let the rain on the bells and the ravens and the smaller birds and the ferns and the trees and the wind fill his ears.

How crazy it had been to wait for the music to start. You

had to supply your own. Make it out of what was there. Because there was more than the rain forest. Beyond his earphones there were people talking, departure announcements, a man waxing the floor—they were all part of the music.

Then suddenly there was a voice much closer.

"Matthew," said the voice, and Matthew became part of the music. "Matthew." Barnsey opened his eyes and his father was sitting there beside him. He touched his son's knee so tentatively, it was as if he was afraid the boy might break, like some fragile ornament from the gift store. Barnsey wondered if he would break, but he wouldn't. He was going to Vancouver to find Dawn. He stared at his father, who could not know this.

His father was in his black coat and white scarf, but his hair was a complete mess. Barnsey had never seen his father out of the house unshaven and looking such a mess. His eyes were the worst mess of all.

"You look scared," said Barnsey. His father nodded. He didn't speak. He was waiting, giving Barnsey space. Then Barnsey looked closer into those wrecked eyes and suddenly it occurred to him that his father wasn't giving him space. He just didn't have any idea what to say or do. He was a million miles from the safe world of the gift store. He looked as if all his careful plans had fallen through.

Barnsey wanted to shake him, to knuckle his head, to throw stuff at him, laughing and shoving. To wake him up.

"Here," he said. He took off his earphones and put them on his father.

"What is it?" his father asked. "Is it broken?"

"No," said Barnsey. "Listen closely."

He watched his father listening. Barnsey listened, too. He didn't need the earphones to hear it.

Beautiful & Cruel

Sandra Cisneros

I am an ugly daughter. I am the one nobody comes for.

Nenny says she won't wait her whole life for a husband to come and get her, that Minerva's sister left her mother's house by having a baby, but she doesn't want to go that way either. She wants things all her own, to pick and choose. Nenny has pretty eyes and it's easy to talk that way if you are pretty.

My mother says when I get older my dusty hair will settle and my blouse will learn to stay clean, but I have decided not to grow up tame like the others who lay their necks on the threshold waiting for the ball and chain.

In the movies there is always one with red red lips who is beautiful and cruel. She is the one who drives the men crazy and laughs them all away. Her power is her own. She will not give it away.

I have begun my own quiet war. Simple. Sure. I am one who leaves the table like a man, without putting back the chair or picking up the plate.

Trip in a Summer Dress

Annette Sanford

119

Moths are already dying under the street lamps when I board the bus. I have said goodbye to my mother and to Matthew, who is crying because he's almost six and knows I won't be back in time for his birthday. I won't be back for the next one either, but who's going to tell him that?

I spread myself out on two seats. I have a brown plastic purse, a tan makeup case, and a paperback book. I could be anybody starting a trip.

The driver is putting the rest of my things in the luggage compartment. His name is E. E. Davis, and the sign at the front of the bus says not to talk to him. He can count on me.

The bus is coughing gray smoke into the loading lanes. I can see my mother and Matthew moving back into the station, out of sight. I fan myself with the paperback and smooth the skirt of my dress. Blue. Cotton. No sleeves.

"It's too late for a summer dress," my mother said while we waited. Before that, she said October is a cold month in Arkansas. She said that Matthew needs vitamins, that the man who sells tickets looks like Uncle Harry. Some things she said twice without even noticing.

We're moving finally.

E. E. Davis is making announcements in a voice like a spoon scraping a cooking pot. *We rest twenty minutes in Huntsville, we stay in our seats while the coach is in motion.* All the time he's talking I'm watching my mother and Matthew on the corner waiting for the light to change. Matthew is sucking two fingers and searching the bus windows for me. I could wave, but I don't.

I'm riding off into the night because two days from now in Eureka Springs, Arkansas, I'm going to be married. Bill Richards is his name. He has brown hair and a gentle touch and a barber shop. He thinks marriages are made in heaven. He thinks Matthew is my mother's son.

She's young enough. She married and had her first child when she was fifteen. So did I, but I wasn't married.

Matthew was born on Uncle Harry's tree farm in East Texas where I went with my mother after she told all her friends she was pregnant again. She needed fresh air and a brother's sympathy, she said, and me to look after her.

Knowing me, maybe some of them believed her.

I was skinny and flat-chested and worked after school in the aviary at the zoo mixing up peanut butter and sunflower seeds and feeding fuzzy orphans with an eye dropper. Most nights I studied. What happened was just a mistake I made because I'd never given much thought to that kind of thing and when the time came it caught me without my mind made up one way or the other.

So we went to the tree farm.

Every day while we waited my mother preached me a sermon: you didn't pass around a child like a piece of cake, and you didn't own him like a house or a refrigerator, and you didn't tell him one thing was true one day and something else was true the next. You took a child and set him down in the safest place you could find. Then you taught him the rules and let him grow. One thing for sure: you didn't come along later just when he was thinking he was a rose and tell him he was a lily instead, just because it suited you to.

What you did was you gave him to your mother and father and you called him your brother and that was that.

Except for one thing. They let you name him.

I picked Matthew because of the dream.

All through that night I'd been Moses' sister tending to the reed basket when the queen found him. All night I was Moses' sister running up and down that river bank hollering till my throat about burst. When the pain was over, there he was—with my mother taking care of him just like the Bible story says. Only you can't name a little pink baby Moses because Moses was mostly an old man. So I settled on Matthew.

It made him mine.

There are four people on this bus. There's a black boy in the second seat blowing bubbles with his gum. Across from him are a couple of ladies just out of the beauty parlor with hair too blue, and a child one seat up across from me. A little girl. Scared probably. She's pretty young for traveling in the dark.

I'm not going to look at them anymore. Everything you do in this life gets mixed up with something else, so you better watch out, even just looking at people. Landscapes are safer.

Pine trees, rice fields, oil rigs. I got my fill of them coming back from Uncle Harry's. I didn't look once at Matthew, but I felt him, even when he wasn't crying. He had hold of me way down deep and wouldn't let go for love nor money.

I sat on the back seat. My father drove and my mother cooed at her brand-new son, the first one in four girls. If she said that one time, she said it a hundred.

Finally I said—so loud my father ran off the road, "He's not your child! I birthed him. I'm his mother, and I'm going to raise him up to know I am! Now what's the matter with that?"

My mother said, "Count the I's, and you'll know." She didn't even turn around.

I got used to it, the way you do a thorn that won't come out or chronic appendicitis. But it's hard to pretend all the time that something's true when it isn't.

So I didn't.

I talked to Matthew about it. I fed him cereal on the back porch by the banana tree, and I told him just how it was he came about. I took him to the park in his red-striped stroller and showed him pansies and tulips and iris blooming. I told him they were beautiful and that's the way it is with love.

Only I hadn't loved his father, I said, and that's where I was wrong. A person ought never to give his body if his soul can't come along.

I told him I'd never leave him because he was me and I was him, and no matter what his mother—who was really his grandmother—said, I had a plan that would save us.

Then he learned to talk, and I had to quit all that.

It's just as well 'cause look at me now. Leaving. Going away from him as hard and fast as ever I can. Me and E. E. Davis burning up the pavement to Huntsville so we can rest twenty minutes and start up again.

Now here's a town.

That little girl across the aisle is rising up and squirm-ing around. Maybe she lives here. Maybe one of those houses going by with lights on and people eating supper inside is hers. But I'm not going to ask. You get a child started talking, you can't stop them sometimes.

Like Matthew.

The day I said yes to Bill Richards I set my plan a-going. I took Matthew to the park like I always had. We sat under a tree where I knew something was likely to happen because lately it always did, and when it started, I said: "Looka there, Matthew. See that redbird feeding her baby?"

"That's not her baby," he said when he finally found the limb. "She's littler than it."

"That's right. The baby's a cowbird, but it *thinks* it's a redbird."

He was real interested. "Does the redbird know it's not her baby?"

"Yes, but she keeps on taking care of it because it hatched in her nest and she loves it."

"How did it get in her nest?"

"Its mama left it there." I'm taking it slow by then, being mighty careful. "She gave it to the redbirds, but just for a little while."

Matthew looked at me. "Mamas don't do that."

"Sometimes they do. If they have to."

"Why would they have to?"

"If they can't take care of the babies, it's better that way."

"Why can't they take care of them?"

"Well. For one thing, cowbirds are too lazy to build nests. Or won't. Or can't." I saw right away I'd said it all wrong.

Matthew stuck out his bottom lip. "I don't like cow-birds."

"They aren't really bad birds," I said quick as I could. "They just got started on the wrong foot—*wing*." Nothing went right with that conversation.

"They're ugly too."

"The mama comes back, Matthew. She always comes back. She whistles and the baby hears and they fly away together."

"I wouldn't go. I'd peck her with my nose."

"Let's go look at the swans," I said.

"I'd tell her to go away and never come back."

"Maybe you'd like some popcorn."

"I would be a redbird forever!"

"Or peanuts. How about a nice big bag?"

When we got home he crawled up in my mother's lap and kissed her a million times. He told her cowbirds are awful. He told her he was mighty glad he belonged to her and not to a cowbird. She was mighty glad too, she said.

I told her now was the time to set things straight and she could be a plenty big help if she wanted to.

She told me little pitchers have big ears.

Eureka Springs is about the size of this town we're going through. In Eureka Springs the barber shop of Bill Richards is set on a mountain corner, he says, and the streets drop off like shelves around it. Eureka Springs is a tourist place. Christ stands on a hill there and sees the goings-on. In Eureka Springs, Bill Richards has a house with window boxes in the front and geraniums growing out, just waiting for someone to pick them.

I can see people in these houses in this town hanging

up coats and opening doors and kissing each other. Women are washing dishes, and kids are getting lessons.

Next year Matthew is going to school in Houston. My mother will walk with him to the corner where he'll catch the bus. He'll have on short pants and a red shirt because red's his favorite color, and he won't want to let go of her hand. In Eureka Springs it will be too cool for a boy to start school wearing short pants.

In Eureka Springs, a boy won't have to.

I can see I was wrong about that little girl. She's not scared. She's been up and down the aisle twice and pestered E. E. Davis. She's gotten chewing gum from the boy and candy from the ladies. It's my turn now, I guess.

"Hello." I know better, but I can't help it.

She puts a sticky hand on my arm. "How come you're crying?"

"Dirt in my eye."

"From the chemical plant," she says, pretty smarty. "They're p'luters. They make plastic bags and umber-ellas."

I open my purse and take out a Kleenex. "How do you know?"

"I know everything on this road."

"You live on it?"

She throws back her head like a TV star. "Prac'ly. Fridays I go that way." She points toward the back window. "Sundays I come back. My daddy's got week-in custardy."

She hangs on the seat in front of me and breathes through her mouth. She smells like corn chips. "They had a big fight, but Mama won most of me. You got any kids?"

"No—yes."

"Don't you know?" A tooth is missing under those pouty lips.

"I have a boy, a little younger than you." I never said it out loud before to anybody but Matthew, and him when he was just a baby.

"Where is he?"

"At home. With his grandmother."

"Whyn't you bring him?"

"I'm going a far piece. He's better off there."

She pops her gum and swings a couple of times on one heel. "You got a boyfriend?"

"Yes." It's out before I can stop it. I ought to bite my tongue off or shake her good. A child with no manners is an abomination before the Lord, my mother says. That's one thing about my mother. She won't let Matthew get away with a thing.

The child turns up her mouth corners, but it's not a smile. "My mama's got one too. Name's Rex. He'g got three gold teeth and a Cadillac."

"How far is it to Huntsville?"

"Two more towns and a dance hall."

"You run on. I'm going to take a nap."

She wanders off up the aisle and plops in a seat. In a second her feet are up in it, her skirt sky-high. Somebody ought to care that she does that. Somebody ought to be here to tell her to sit up like a lady. Especially on a bus. All kinds of people ride buses.

I met Bill Richards on a bus. Going to Galveston for Splash Day. He helped us off and carried my tote bag and bought us hot dogs. He bought Matthew a snow cone. He built him a castle. He gave him a shoulder ride right into the waves. A girl married to Bill Richards wouldn't have to do a thing but love him.

A girl married to Bill Richards wouldn't tell him she

had a son with no father, my mother said. And she wouldn't tell her son he was her son. Or a redbird either. She would forget it and love her brother.

We're stopping at a filling station sort of place. The blue-haired ladies are tying nets around their heads and stuffing things in paper sacks. They get out and a lot of hot air comes in. The door pops shut and E. E. Davis gives it the gas. "Ten more miles to Huntsville."

"My mama better be there this time!" the child says, loud and quivery. I had it right in the first place, I guess. Her scare is just all slicked over with chewing gum and smart talk. Inside she's powerful shaky.

"Your mama'll be there, don't you worry." Before I can close my mouth she's on me like a plaster cast. I should have been a missionary.

"She's always late. Last time I waited all night. The bus station man bought me a cheese sandwich and covered me up with his coat."

"Something kept her, I guess."

"Yeah." She slides down in the seat beside me. "Rex."

I don't want to talk to her. I want to think about things. I want to figure out how it's going to be in Eureka Springs with Christ looking right into the kitchen window when I'm kissing Bill Richards, and Him knowing all the time about Moses' sister. I want to think about Matthew growing up and getting married himself and even dying without ever knowing I'm his mother.

Most of all I want to get off this bus and go and get my baby.

"Huntsville!" yells E. E.

"I told you! I told you she wouldn't be here." That child's got a grip on my left hand so tight the blood's quit running. We're standing in the waiting room with lots of faces, but none of them is the right one. It's pitch dark outside and hot as a devil's poker.

"Just sit down," I say. "She'll come."

"I have to go to the bathroom."

"Go ahead. I'll watch for her."

I go in the phone booth. No matter what my mother says, Matthew is a big boy. He can take it. So can Bill Richards. I put two quarters and seven nickels on the shelf by the receiver. I get the dial tone. I spin the numbers out, eleven of them, and drop my money in the slot.

I see the woman coming in out of the dark. She's holding hands with a gold-toothed man and her mouth's all pouty like the child's. My mother's voice shouts hello in my ear.

"Wait," I tell her.

I open the door of the phone booth. "Wait! She's in the restroom. Your child. There, she's coming yonder."

I can see they wish she wasn't. I can see how they hate Sundays.

"Talk if you're going to," my mother says. She only calls long distance when somebody dies.

"Mama, I wanted to tell you—"

"That you wish you had your coat. I knew it! The air's too still and sticky not to be breeding a blizzard."

"It's *hot* here, for goodness sakes!"

"Won't be for long. Thirty by morning the TV says. Twenty where you're going. Look in the makeup case. I stuck in your blue wool sweater."

"Matthew—"

"In bed and finally dropping off. I told him an hour ago, the sooner you shed today, the quicker tomorrow'll come, but he's something else to convince, that boy."

"Comes by it naturally," I say, and plenty loud, but she doesn't hear.

"Have a good trip," she's yelling, "and wrap up warm in the wind."

When I step outside, it's blowing all right, just like she said. Hard from the north and sharp as a scissors.

By the time E. E. Davis swings open the door and bellows, "All aboard for Eureka Springs," that wind is tossing up newspapers and bus drivers' caps and hems of summer dresses. It's whipping through door cracks and rippling puddles and freezing my arms where the sleeves ought to be.

If I was my mother, I'd get mighty tired of always being right.

On the Rainy River

Tim O'Brien

This is one story I've never told before. Not to anyone. Not to my parents, not to my brother or sister, not even to my wife. To go into it, I've always thought, would only cause embarrassment for all of us, a sudden need to be elsewhere, which is the natural response to a confession. Even now, I'll admit, the story makes me squirm. For more than twenty years I've had to live with it, feeling the shame, trying to push it away, and so by this act of remembrance, by putting the facts down on paper, I'm hoping to relieve at least some of the pressure on my dreams. Still, it's a hard story to tell. All of us, I suppose, like to believe that in a moral emergency we will behave like the heroes of our youth, bravely and forthrightly, without thought of personal loss or discredit. Certainly that was my conviction back in the summer of 1968. Tim O'Brien: a secret hero. The Lone Ranger. If the stakes ever became high enough—if the evil were evil enough, if the good were good enough—I would simply tap a secret reservoir of courage that had been accumulating inside me over the years. Courage, I seemed to think, comes to us in finite quantities, like an inheritance, and by being frugal and stashing it away and letting it earn interest, we steadily increase our moral capital in preparation for that day when the account must be drawn down. It was a comforting theory. It dispensed with all those bothersome little acts of daily courage; it offered hope and grace to the repetitive coward; it justified the past while amortizing the future.

In June of 1968, a month after graduating from Macalester College, I was drafted to fight a war I hated. I was twenty-one years old. Young, yes, and politically naive, but even so the American war in Vietnam seemed to me wrong. Certain blood was being shed for uncertain reasons. I saw no unity of purpose, no consensus on matters of philosophy or history or law. The very facts were shrouded in uncertainty: Was it a civil war? A war of national liberation or simple aggression? Who started it, and when, and why? What really happened to the USS *Maddox* on that dark night in the Gulf of Tonkin? Was Ho Chi Minh a Communist stooge, or a nationalist savior, or both, or neither? What about the Geneva Accords? What about SEATO and the Cold War? What about dominoes? America was divided on these and a thousand other issues, and the debate had spilled out across the floor of the United States Senate and into the streets, and smart men in pinstripes could not agree on even the most fundamental matters of public policy. The only certainty that summer was moral confusion. It was my view then, and still is, that you don't make war without knowing why. Knowledge, of course, is always imperfect, but it seemed to me that when a nation goes to war it must have reasonable confidence in the justice and imperative of its cause. You can't fix your mistakes. Once people are dead, you can't make them undead.

In any case those were my convictions, and back in

college I had taken a modest stand against the war. Nothing radical, no hothead stuff, just ringing a few doorbells for Gene McCarthy, composing a few tedious, uninspired editorials for the campus newspaper. Oddly, though, it was almost entirely an intellectual activity. I brought some energy to it, of course, but it was the energy that accompanies almost any abstract endeavor; I felt no personal danger; I felt no sense of an impending crisis in my life. Stupidly, with a kind of smug removal that I can't begin to fathom, I assumed that the problems of killing and dying did not fall within my special province.

The draft notice arrived on June 17, 1968. It was a humid afternoon, I remember, cloudy and very quiet, and I'd just come in from a round of golf. My mother and father were having lunch out in the kitchen. I remember opening up the letter, scanning the first few lines, feeling the blood go thick behind my eyes. I remember a sound in my head. It wasn't thinking, it was just a silent howl. A million things all at once—I was too *good* for this war. Too smart, too compassionate, too everything. It couldn't happen. I was above it. I had the world dicked—Phi Beta Kappa and summa cum laude and president of the student body and a full-ride scholarship for grad studies at Harvard. A mistake, maybe—a foul-up in the paperwork. I was no soldier. I hated Boy Scouts. I hated camping out. I hated dirt and tents and mosquitoes. The sight of blood made me queasy, and I couldn't tolerate authority, and I didn't know a rifle from a slingshot. I was a *liberal*, for Christ sake: If they needed fresh bodies, why not draft some back-to-the-stone-age hawk? Or some dumb jingo in his hard hat and Bomb Hanoi button? Or one of LBJ's pretty daughters? Or Westmoreland's whole family—nephews and nieces and baby grandson? There should be a law, I thought. If you support a war, if you think it's worth the price, that's fine, but you have to put your own life on the line. You have to head for the front and hook up with an infantry unit and help spill the blood. And you have to bring along your wife, or your kids, or your lover. A *law*, I thought.

I remember the rage in my stomach. Later it burned down to a smoldering self-pity, then to numbness. At dinner that night my father asked what my plans were.

"Nothing," I said. "Wait."

I spent the summer of 1968 working in an Armour meat-packing plant in my hometown of Worthington, Minnesota. The plant specialized in pork products, and for eight hours a day I stood on a quarter-mile assembly line—more properly, a disassembly line—removing blood clots from the necks of dead pigs. My job title, I believe, was Declotter. After slaughter, the hogs were decapitated, split down the length of the belly, pried open, eviscerated, and strung up by the hind hocks on a high conveyer belt. Then gravity took over. By the time a carcass reached my spot on the line, the fluids had mostly drained out, everything except for thick clots of blood in the neck and upper chest cavity. To remove the stuff, I used a kind of water gun. The machine was heavy, maybe eighty pounds, and was suspended from the ceiling by a heavy rubber cord. There was some bounce to it, an elastic up-and-down give, and the trick was to maneuver the gun with your whole body, not lifting with the arms, just letting the rubber cord do the work for you. At one end was a trigger; at the muzzle end was a small nozzle and a steel roller brush. As a carcass passed by, you'd lean forward and swing the gun up against the clots and squeeze the trigger, all in one motion, and the brush would whirl and water would come shooting out and you'd hear a quick splattering sound as the clots dissolved into a fine red mist. It was not pleasant work. Goggles were a necessity, and a rubber apron, but even so it was like standing for eight hours a day under a lukewarm blood-shower. At night I'd go home smelling of pig. I couldn't wash it out. Even after a hot bath, scrubbing hard, the stink was always there—like old bacon, or sausage, a dense greasy pig-stink that soaked deep into my skin and hair. Among other things, I remember, it was tough getting dates that summer. I felt isolated; I spent a lot of time alone. And there was also that draft notice tucked away in my wallet.

In the evenings I'd sometimes borrow my father's car and drive aimlessly around town, feeling sorry for myself, thinking about the war and the pig factory and how my life seemed to be collapsing toward slaughter. I felt paralyzed. All around me the options seemed to be narrowing, as if I were hurtling down a huge black funnel, the whole world squeezing in tight. There was no happy way out. The government had ended most graduate school deferments; the waiting lists for the National Guard and Reserves were impossibly long; my health was solid; I didn't qualify for CO status—no religious grounds, no history as a pacifist. Moreover, I could not claim to be opposed to war as a matter of general principle. There were occasions, I believed, when a nation was justified in using military force to achieve its ends, to stop a Hitler or some comparable evil, and I told myself that in such circumstances I would've willingly marched off to the battle. The problem, though, was that a draft board did not let you choose your war.

Beyond all this, or at the very center, was the raw fact of terror. I did not want to die. Not ever. But certainly not then, not there, not in a wrong war. Driving up Main Street, past the courthouse and the Ben Franklin store, I sometimes felt the fear spreading inside me like weeds. I imagined myself dead. I imagined myself doing things I could not do—charging an enemy position, taking aim at another human being.

At some point in mid-July I began thinking seriously about Canada. The border lay a few hundred miles north, an eight-hour drive. Both my conscience and my instincts were telling me to make a break for it, just take off and run like hell and never stop. In the beginning the idea seemed purely abstract, the word Canada printing itself out in my head; but after a time I could see particular shapes and images, the sorry details of my own future—a hotel room in Winnipeg, a battered old suitcase, my father's eyes as I tried to explain myself over the telephone. I could almost hear his voice, and my mother's. Run, I'd think. Then I'd think, Impossible. Then a second later I'd think, *Run*.

It was a kind of schizophrenia. A moral split. I couldn't make up my mind. I feared the war, yes, but I also feared exile. I was afraid of walking away from my own life, my friends and my family, my whole history, everything that mattered to me. I feared losing the respect of my parents. I feared the law. I feared ridicule and censure. My hometown was a conservative little spot on the prairie, a place where tradition counted, and it was easy to imagine people sitting around a table down at the old Gobbler Café on Main Street, coffee cups poised, the conversation slowly zeroing in on the young O'Brien kid, how the damned sissy had taken off for Canada. At night, when I couldn't sleep,

I'd sometimes carry on fierce arguments with those people. I'd be screaming at them, telling them how much I detested their blind, thoughtless, automatic acquiescence to it all, their simple-minded patriotism, their prideful ignorance, their love-it-or-leave-it platitudes, how they were sending me off to fight a war they didn't understand and didn't want to understand. I held them responsible. By God, yes, I *did*. All of them—I held them personally and individually responsible—the polyestered Kiwanis boys, the merchants and farmers, the pious churchgoers, the chatty housewives, the PTA and the Lions club and the Veterans of Foreign Wars and the fine upstanding gentry out at the country club. They didn't know Bao Dai from the man in the moon. They didn't know history. They didn't know the first thing about Diem's tyranny, or the nature of Vietnamese nationalism, or the long colonialism of the French—this was all too damned complicated, it required some reading—but no matter, it was a war to stop the Communists, plain and simple, which was how they liked things, and you were a treasonous pussy if you had second thoughts about killing or dying for plain and simple reasons.

I was bitter, sure. But it was so much more than that. The emotions went from outrage to terror to bewilderment to guilt to sorrow and then back again to outrage. I felt a sickness inside me. Real disease.

Most of this I've told before, or at least hinted at, but what I have never told is the full truth. How I cracked. How at work one morning, standing on the pig line, I felt something break open in my chest. I don't know what it was. I'll never know. But it was real, I know that much, it was a physical rupture—a cracking-leaking-popping feeling. I remember dropping my water gun. Quickly, almost without thought, I took off my apron and walked out of the plant and drove home. It was midmorning, I remember, and the house was empty. Down in my chest there was still that leaking sensation, something very warm and precious spilling out, and I was covered with blood and hog-stink, and for a long while I just concentrated on holding myself together. I remember taking a hot shower. I remember packing a suitcase and carrying it out to the kitchen, standing very still for a few minutes, looking carefully at the familiar objects all around me. The old chrome toaster, the telephone, the pink and white Formica on the kitchen counters. The room was full of bright sunshine. Everything sparkled. My house, I thought. My life. I'm not sure how long I stood there, but later I scribbled out a short note to my parents.

What it said, exactly, I don't recall now. Something vague. Taking off, will call, love Tim.

I drove north.

It's a blur now, as it was then, and all I remember is a sense of high velocity and the feel of the steering wheel in my hands. I was riding on adrenaline. A giddy feeling, in a way, except there was the dreamy edge of impossibility to it—like running a dead-end maze—no way out—it couldn't come to a happy conclusion and yet I was doing it anyway because it was all I could think of to do. It was pure flight, fast and mindless. I had no plan. Just hit the border at high speed and crash through and keep on running. Near dusk I passed through Bemidji, then turned northeast toward International Falls. I spent the night in the car behind a closed-down gas station a half mile from the border. In the morning, after gassing up, I headed straight west along the Rainy River, which separates Minnesota from Canada, and which for me separated one life from another. The land was mostly wilderness. Here and there I passed a motel or bait shop, but otherwise the country unfolded in great sweeps of pine and birch and sumac. Though it was still August, the air already had the smell of October, football season, piles of yellow-red leaves, everything crisp and clean. I remember a huge blue sky. Off to my right was the Rainy River, wide as a lake in places, and beyond the Rainy River was Canada.

For a while I just drove, not aiming at anything, then in the late morning I began looking for a place to lie low for a day or two. I was exhausted, and scared sick, and around noon I pulled into an old fishing resort called the Tip Top Lodge. Actually it was not a lodge at all, just eight or nine tiny yellow cabins clustered on a peninsula that jutted northward into the Rainy River. The place was in sorry shape. There was a dangerous wooden dock, an old minnow tank, a flimsy tar paper boathouse along the shore. The main building, which stood in a cluster of pines on high ground, seemed to lean heavily to one side, like a cripple, the roof sagging toward Canada. Briefly, I thought about turning around, just giving up, but then I got out of the car and walked up to the front porch.

The man who opened the door that day is the hero of my life. How do I say this without sounding sappy? Blurt it out—the man saved me. He offered exactly what I needed, without questions, without any words at all. He took me in. He was there at the critical time—a silent, watchful presence. Six days later, when it ended, I was unable to find a proper way to thank him, and I never have, and so, if nothing else, this story represents a small gesture of gratitude twenty years overdue.

Even after two decades I can close my eyes and return
to that porch at the Tip Top Lodge. I can see the old guy
staring at me. Elroy Berdahl: eighty-one years old, skinny
and shrunken and mostly bald. He wore a flannel shirt and
brown work pants. In one hand, I remember, he carried a
green apple, a small paring knife in the other. His eyes had
the bluish gray color of a razor blade, the same polished
shine, and as he peered up at me I felt a strange sharpness,
almost painful, a cutting sensation, as if his gaze were
somehow slicing me open. In part, no doubt, it was my own
sense of guilt, but even so I'm absolutely certain that the
old man took one look and went right to the heart of
things—a kid in trouble. When I asked for a room, Elroy
made a little clicking sound with his tongue. He nodded,
led me out to one of the cabins, and dropped a key in my
hand. I remember smiling at him. I also remember wishing
I hadn't. The old man shook his head as if to tell me it
wasn't worth the bother.

"Dinner at five-thirty," he said. "You eat fish?"

"Anything," I said.

Elroy grunted and said, "I'll bet."

We spent six days together at the Tip Top Lodge. Just the
two of us. Tourist season was over, and there were no boats
on the river, and the wilderness seemed to withdraw into
a great permanent stillness. Over those six days Elroy
Berdahl and I took most of our meals together. In the
mornings we sometimes went out on long hikes into the
woods, and at night we played Scrabble or listened to
records or sat reading in front of his big stone fireplace. At

times I felt the awkwardness of an intruder, but Elroy accepted me into his quiet routine without fuss or ceremony. He took my presence for granted, the same way he might've sheltered a stray cat—no wasted sighs or pity—and there was never any talk about it. Just the opposite. What I remember more than anything is the man's willful, almost ferocious silence. In all that time together, all those hours, he never asked the obvious questions: Why was I there? Why alone? Why so preoccupied? If Elroy was curious about any of this, he was careful never to put it into words.

My hunch, though, is that he already knew. At least the basics. After all, it was 1968, and guys were burning draft cards, and Canada was just a boat ride away. Elroy Berdahl was no hick. His bedroom, I remember, was cluttered with books and newspapers. He killed me at the Scrabble board, barely concentrating, and on those occasions when speech was necessary he had a way of compressing large thoughts into small, cryptic packets of language. One evening, just at sunset, he pointed up at an owl circling over the violet-lighted forest to the west.

"Hey, O'Brien," he said. "There's Jesus."

The man was sharp—he didn't miss much. Those razor eyes. Now and then he'd catch me staring out at the river, at the far shore, and I could almost hear the tumblers clicking in his head. Maybe I'm wrong, but I doubt it.

One thing for certain, he knew I was in desperate trouble. And he knew I couldn't talk about it. The wrong word—or even the right word—and I would've disappeared. I was wired and jittery. My skin felt too tight. After supper one evening I vomited and went back to my cabin and lay down for a few moments and then vomited again;

Tim O'Brien

another time, in the middle of the afternoon, I began sweating and couldn't shut it off. I went through whole days feeling dizzy with sorrow. I couldn't sleep; I couldn't lie still. At night I'd toss around in bed, half awake, half dreaming, imagining how I'd sneak down to the beach and quietly push one of the old man's boats out into the river and start paddling my way toward Canada. There were times when I thought I'd gone off the psychic edge. I couldn't tell up from down, I was just falling, and late in the night I'd lie there watching weird pictures spin through my head. Getting chased by the Border Patrol—helicopters and searchlights and barking dogs—I'd be crashing through the woods, I'd be down on my hands and knees—people shouting out my name—the law closing in on all sides—my hometown draft board and the FBI and the Royal Canadian Mounted Police. It all seemed crazy and impossible. Twenty-one years old, an ordinary kid with all the ordinary dreams and ambitions, and all I wanted was to live the life I was born to—a mainstream life—I loved baseball and hamburgers and cherry Cokes—and now I was off on the margins of exile, leaving my country forever, and it seemed so impossible and terrible and sad.

I'm not sure how I made it through those six days. Most of it I can't remember. On two or three afternoons, to pass some time, I helped Elroy get the place ready for winter, sweeping down the cabins and hauling in the boats, little chores that kept my body moving. The days were cool and bright. The nights were very dark. One morning the old man showed me how to split and stack firewood, and for several hours we just worked in silence out behind his house. At one point, I remember, Elroy put down his maul and looked at me for a long time, his lips drawn as if framing a difficult question, but then he shook his head and went back to work. The man's self-control was amazing. He never pried. He never put me in a position that required lies or denials. To an extent, I suppose, his reticence was typical of that part of Minnesota, where privacy still held value, and even if I'd been walking around with some horrible deformity—four arms and three heads—I'm sure the old man would've talked about everything except those extra arms and heads. Simple politeness was part of it. But even more than that, I think, the man understood that words were insufficient. The problem had gone beyond discussion. During that long summer I'd been over and over the various arguments, all the pros and cons, and it was no longer a question that could be decided by an act of pure reason. Intellect had come up against emotion. My conscience told me to run, but some irrational and powerful force was resisting, like a weight pushing me toward the war. What it came down to, stupidly, was a sense of shame. Hot, stupid shame. I did not want people to think badly of me. Not my parents, not my brother and sister, not even the folks down at the Gobbler Café. I was ashamed to be there at the Tip Top Lodge. I was ashamed of my conscience, ashamed to be doing the right thing.

Some of this Elroy must've understood. Not the details, of course, but the plain fact of crisis.

Although the old man never confronted me about it, there was one occasion when he came close to forcing the whole thing out into the open. It was early evening, and we'd just finished supper, and over coffee and dessert I asked him about my bill, how much I owed so far. For a long while the old man squinted down at the tablecloth.

"Well, the basic rate," he said, "is fifty bucks a night.

Not counting meals. This makes four nights, right?"

I nodded. I had three hundred and twelve dollars in my wallet.

Elroy kept his eyes on the tablecloth. "Now that's an on-season price. To be fair, I suppose we should knock it down a peg or two." He leaned back in his chair. "What's a reasonable number, you figure?"

"I don't know," I said. "Forty?"

"Forty's good. Forty a night. Then we tack on food— say another hundred? Two hundred sixty total?"

"I guess."

He raised his eyebrows. "Too much?"

"No, that's fair. It's fair. Tomorrow, though . . . I think I'd better take off tomorrow."

Elroy shrugged and began clearing the table. For a time he fussed with the dishes, whistling to himself as if the subject had been settled. After a second he slapped his hands together.

"You know what we forgot?" he said. "We forgot wages. Those odd jobs you done. What we have to do, we have to figure out what your time's worth. Your last job—how much did you pull in an hour?"

"Not enough," I said.

"A bad one?"

"Yes. Pretty bad."

Slowly then, without intending any long sermon, I told him about my days at the pig plant. It began as a straight recitation of the facts, but before I could stop myself I was talking about the blood clots and the water gun and how the smell had soaked into my skin and how I couldn't wash it away. I went on for a long time. I told him about wild hogs squealing in my dreams, the sounds of butchery, slaughterhouse sounds, and how I'd sometimes wake up with that greasy pig-stink in my throat.

When I was finished, Elroy nodded at me.

"Well, to be honest," he said, "when you first showed up here, I wondered about all that. The aroma, I mean. Smelled like you was awful damned fond of pork chops." The old man almost smiled. He made a snuffling sound, then sat down with a pencil and a piece of paper. "So what'd this crud job pay? Ten bucks an hour? Fifteen?"

"Less."

Elroy shook his head. "Let's make it fifteen. You put in twenty-five hours here, easy. That's three hundred seventy-five bucks total wages. We subtract the two hundred sixty for food and lodging, I still owe you a hundred and fifteen."

He took four fifties out of his shirt pocket and laid them on the table.

"Call it even," he said.

"No."

"Pick it up. Get yourself a haircut."

The money lay on the table for the rest of the evening. It was still there when I went back to my cabin. In the morning, though, I found an envelope tacked to my door. Inside were the four fifties and a two-word note that said EMERGENCY FUND.

The man knew.

Looking back after twenty years, I sometimes wonder if the events of that summer didn't happen in some other dimension, a place where your life exists before you've lived it, and where it goes afterward. None of it ever seemed real. During my time at the Tip Top Lodge I had the feeling that I'd slipped out of my own skin, hovering a few feet away while some poor yo-yo with my name and face tried to make his way toward a future he didn't understand and didn't want. Even now I can see myself as I was then. It's like watching an old home movie: I'm young and tan and fit. I've got hair—lots of it. I don't smoke or drink. I'm wearing faded blue jeans and a white polo shirt. I can see myself sitting on Elroy Berdahl's dock near dusk one evening, the sky a bright shimmering pink, and I'm finishing up a letter to my parents that tells what I'm about to do and why I'm doing it and how sorry I am that I'd never found the courage to talk to them about it. I ask them not to be angry. I try to explain some of my feelings, but there aren't enough words, and so I just say that it's a thing that has to be done. At the end of the letter I talk about the vacations we used to take up in this north country, at a place called Whitefish Lake, and how the scenery here reminds me of those good times. I tell them I'm fine. I tell them I'll write again from Winnipeg or Montreal or wherever I end up.

On my last full day, the sixth day, the old man took me out fishing on the Rainy River. The afternoon was sunny and cold. A still breeze came in from the north, and I remember how the little fourteen-foot boat made sharp rocking motions as we pushed off from the dock. The current was fast. All around us, I remember, there was a vastness to the world, an unpeopled rawness, just the trees and the sky and the water reaching out toward nowhere. The air had the brittle scent of October.

For ten or fifteen minutes Elroy held a course upstream, the river choppy and silver-gray, then he turned straight north and put the engine on full throttle. I felt the bow lift beneath me. I remember the wind in my ears, the sound of the old outboard Evinrude. For a time I didn't pay attention to anything, just feeling the cold spray against my face, but then it occurred to me that at some point we must've passed into Canadian waters, across that dotted line between two different worlds, and I remember a sudden tightness in my chest as I looked up and watched the far shore come at me. This wasn't a daydream. It was tangible and real. As we came in toward land, Elroy cut the engine, letting the boat fishtail lightly about twenty yards off shore. The old man didn't look at me or speak. Bending down, he opened up his tackle box and busied himself with a bobber and a piece of wire leader, humming to himself, his eyes down.

It struck me then that he must've planned it. I'll never be certain, of course, but I think he meant to bring me up against the realities, to guide me across the river and to take me to the edge and to stand a kind of vigil as I chose a life for myself.

I remember staring at the old man, then at my hands, then at Canada. The shoreline was dense with brush and timber. I could see tiny red berries on the bushes. I could see a squirrel up in one of the birch trees, a big crow looking at me from a boulder along the river. That close— twenty yards—and I could see the delicate latticework of the leaves, the texture of the soil, the browned needles beneath the pines, the configurations of geology and human history. Twenty yards. I could've done it. I could've jumped and started swimming for my life. Inside me, in my chest, I felt a terrible squeezing pressure. Even now, as I write this, I can still feel that tightness. And I want you to feel it—the wind coming off the river, the waves, the silence, the wooded frontier. You're at the bow of a boat on the Rainy River. You're twenty-one years old, you're scared, and there's a hard squeezing pressure in your chest.

What would you do?

Would you jump? Would you feel pity for yourself? Would you think about your family and your childhood and your dreams and all you're leaving behind? Would it hurt? Would it feel like dying? Would you cry, as I did?

I tried to swallow it back. I tried to smile, except I was crying.

Now, perhaps, you can understand why I've never told this story before. It's not just the embarrassment of tears. That's part of it, no doubt, but what embarrasses me much more, and always will, is the paralysis that took my heart. A moral freeze: I couldn't decide, I couldn't act, I couldn't comport myself with even a pretense of modest human dignity.

All I could do was cry. Quietly, not bawling, just the chest-chokes.

At the rear of the boat Elroy Berdahl pretended not to notice. He held a fishing rod in his hands, his head bowed to hide his eyes. He kept humming a soft, monotonous little tune. Everywhere, it seemed, in the trees and water and sky, a great worldwide sadness came pressing down on me, a crushing sorrow, sorrow like I had never known it before. And what was so sad, I realized, was that Canada had become a pitiful fantasy. Silly and hopeless. It was no longer a possibility. Right then, with the shore so close, I understood that I would not do what I should do. I would not swim away from my hometown and my country and my life. I would not be brave. That old image of myself as a hero, as a man of conscience and courage, all that was just a threadbare pipe dream. Bobbing there on the Rainy River, looking back at the Minnesota shore, I felt a sudden swell of helplessness come over me, a drowning sensation, as if I had toppled overboard and was being swept away by the silver waves. Chunks of my own history flashed by. I saw a seven-year-old boy in a white cowboy hat and a Lone Ranger mask and a pair of holstered six-shooters; I saw a twelve-year-old Little League shortstop pivoting to turn a double play; I saw a sixteen-year-old kid decked out for his first prom, looking spiffy in a white tux and a black bow tie, his hair cut short and flat, his shoes freshly polished. My whole life seemed to spill out into the river, swirling away from me, everything I had ever been or ever wanted to be. I couldn't get my breath; I couldn't stay afloat; I couldn't tell which way to swim. A hallucination, I suppose, but it was as real as anything I would ever feel. I saw my parents calling to me from the far shoreline. I saw my brother and sister, all the townsfolk, the mayor and the entire Chamber of Commerce and all my old teachers and girlfriends and high school buddies. Like some weird sporting event: everybody screaming from the sidelines, rooting me on—a loud stadium roar. Hotdogs and popcorn—stadium smells, stadium heat. A squad of cheerleaders did cartwheels along the banks of the Rainy River; they had megaphones and pompoms and smooth brown thighs. The crowd swayed left and right. A marching band played fight songs. All my aunts and uncles were there, and Abraham Lincoln, and Saint George, and a nine-year-old girl named Linda who had died of a brain tumor back in fifth grade, and several members of the United States Senate, and a blind poet scribbling notes, and LBJ, and Huck Finn, and Abbie Hoffman, and all the dead soldiers back from the grave, and the many thousands who were later to die—villagers with terrible burns, little kids without arms or legs—yes, and the Joint Chiefs of Staff were there, and a couple of popes, and a first lieutenant named Jimmy Cross, and the last surviving veteran of the American Civil War, and Jane Fonda dressed up as Barbarella, and an old man sprawled beside a pigpen, and my grandfather, and Gary Cooper, and a kind-faced woman carrying an umbrella and a copy of Plato's *Republic*, and a million ferocious citizens waving flags of all shapes and colors—people in hard hats, people in headbands— they were all whooping and chanting and urging me toward one shore or the other. I saw faces from my distant past and distant future. My wife was there. My unborn daughter waved at me, and my two sons hopped up and down, and a drill sergeant named Blyton sneered and shot up a finger and shook his head. There was a choir in bright purple robes. There was a cabbie from the Bronx. There was a slim young man I would one day kill with a hand grenade along a red clay trail outside the village of My Khe.

The little aluminum boat rocked softly beneath me. There was the wind and the sky.

I tried to will myself overboard.

I gripped the edge of the boat and leaned forward and thought, *Now.*

I did try. It just wasn't possible.

All those eyes on me—the town, the whole universe— and I couldn't risk the embarrassment. It was as if there were an audience to my life, that swirl of faces along the river, and in my head I could hear people screaming at me. Traitor! they yelled. Turncoat! Pussy! I felt myself blush. I couldn't tolerate it. I couldn't endure the mockery, or the disgrace, or the patriotic ridicule. Even in my imagination, the shore just twenty yards away, I couldn't make myself be brave. It had nothing to do with morality. Embarrassment, that's all it was.

And right then I submitted.

I would go to the war—I would kill and maybe die— because I was embarrassed not to.

That was the sad thing. And so I sat in the bow of the boat and cried.

It was loud now. Loud, hard crying.

Elroy Berdahl remained quiet. He kept fishing. He worked his line with the tips of his fingers, patiently, squinting out at his red and white bobber on the Rainy River. His eyes were flat and impassive. He didn't speak. He was simply there, like the river and the late-summer sun. And yet by his presence, his mute watchfulness, he made it real. He was the true audience. He was a witness, like God, or like the gods, who look on in absolute silence as we live our lives, as we make our choices or fail to make them.

"Ain't biting," he said.

Then after a time the old man pulled in his line and turned the boat back toward Minnesota.

I don't remember saying goodbye. That last night we had dinner together, and I went to bed early, and in the morning Elroy fixed breakfast for me. When I told him I'd be leaving, the old man nodded as if he already knew. He looked down at the table and smiled.

At some point later in the morning it's possible that we shook hands—I just don't remember—but I do know that by the time I'd finished packing the old man had disappeared. Around noon, when I took my suitcase out to the car, I noticed that his old black pickup truck was no longer parked in front of the house. I went inside and waited for a while, but I felt a bone certainty that he wouldn't be back. In a way, I thought, it was appropriate. I washed up the breakfast dishes, left his two hundred dollars on the kitchen counter, got into the car, and drove south toward home.

The day was cloudy. I passed through towns with familiar names, through the pine forests and down to the prairie, and then to Vietnam, where I was a soldier, and then home again. I survived, but it's not a happy ending. I was a coward. I went to the war.

The Setting Sun and the Rolling World

Charles Mungoshi

Old Musoni raised his dusty eyes from his hoe and the unchanging stony earth he had been tilling and peered into the sky. The white speck whose sound had disturbed his work and thoughts was far out at the edge of the yellow sky, near the horizon. Then it disappeared quickly over the southern rim of the sky and he shook his head. He looked to the west. Soon the sun would go down. He looked over the sunblasted land and saw the shadows creeping east, blearer and taller with every moment that the sun shed each of its rays. Unconsciously wishing for rain and relief, he bent down again to his work and did not see his son, Nhamo, approaching.

Nhamo crouched in the dust near his father and greeted him. The old man half raised his back, leaning against his hoe, and said what had been bothering him all day long.

"You haven't changed your mind?"

"No, father."

There was a moment of silence. Old Musoni scraped earth off his hoe.

"Have you thought about this, son?"

"For weeks, father."

"And you think that's the only way?"

"There is no other way."

The old man felt himself getting angry again. But this would be the last day he would talk to his son. If his son was going away, he must not be angry. It would be equal to a curse. He himself had taken chances before, in his own time, but he felt too much of a father. He had worked and slaved for his family and the land had not betrayed him. He saw nothing now but disaster and death for his son out there in the world. Lions had long since vanished but he knew of worse animals of prey, animals that wore redder claws than the lion's, beasts that would not leave an unprotected homeless boy alone. He thought of the white metal bird and he felt remorse.

"Think again. You will end dead. Think again, of us, of your family. We have a home, poor though it is, but can you think of a day you have gone without?"

"I have thought everything over, father, I am convinced this is the only way out."

"There is no only way out in the world. Except the way of the land, the way of the family."

"The land is overworked and gives nothing now, father. And the family is almost broken up."

The old man got angry. Yes, the land is useless. True, the family tree is uprooted and it dries in the sun. True, many things are happening that haven't happened before, that we did not think would happen, ever. But nothing is more certain to hold you together than the land and a home, a family. And where do you think you are going, a mere beardless kid with the milk not yet dry on your baby nose? What do you think you will do in the great treacherous world where men twice your age have gone and returned with their backs broken—if they returned at all? What do you know of life? What do you know of the false honey bird that leads you the whole day through the forest to a snake's nest? But all he said was: "Look. What have you asked me and I have denied you? What, that I have, have I not given you for the asking?"

"All. You have given me all, father." And here, too, the son felt hampered, patronized and his pent-up fury rolled through him. It showed on his face but stayed under control. You have given me damn all and nothing. You have sent me to school and told me the importance of education, and now you ask me to throw it on the rubbish heap and scrape for a living on this tired cold shell of the moon. You ask me to forget it and muck around in this slow dance of death with you. I have this one chance of making my own life, once in all eternity, and now you are jealous. You are afraid of your own death. It is, after all, your own death. I shall be around a while yet. I will make my way home if a home is what I need. I am armed more than you think and wiser than you can dream of. But all he said, too, was:

"Really, father, have no fear for me. I will be all right. Give me this chance. Release me from all obligations and pray for me."

There was a spark in the old man's eyes at these words of his son. But just as dust quickly settles over a glittering pebble revealed by the hoe, so a murkiness hid the gleam in the old man's eye. Words are handles made to the smith's fancy and are liable to break under stress. They are too much fat on the hard unbreaking sinews of life.

"Do you know what you are doing, son?"

"Yes."

"Do you know what you will be a day after you leave home?"

"Yes, father."

"A homeless, nameless vagabond living on dust and rat's droppings, living on thank-yous, sleeping up a tree or down a ditch, in the rain, in the sun, in the cold, with nobody to see you, nobody to talk to, nobody at all to tell your dreams to. Do you know what it is to see your hopes come crashing down like an old house out of season and your dreams turning to ash and dung without a tang of salt in your skull? Do you know what it is to live without a single hope of ever seeing good in your own lifetime?" And to himself: Do you know, young bright ambitious son of my loins, the ruins of time and the pains of old age? Do you know how to live beyond a dream, a hope, a faith? Have you seen black despair, my son?

"I know it, father. I know enough to start on. The rest I shall learn as I go on. Maybe I shall learn to come back."

The old man looked at him and felt: Come back where? Nobody comes back to ruins. You will go on, son. Something you don't know will drive you on along deserted plains, past ruins and more ruins, on and on until there is only one ruin left: yourself. You will break down, without tears, son. You are human, too. Learn to the *haya*—the rain bird, and heed its warning of coming storm: plough no more, it says. And what happens if the storm catches you far, far out on the treeless plain? What, then, my son?

But he was tired. They had taken over two months discussing all this. Going over the same ground like animals at a drinking place until, like animals, they had driven the water far deep into the stony earth, until they had sapped all the blood out of life and turned it into a grim skeleton, and now they were creating a stampede on the dust, groveling for water. Mere thoughts. Mere words. And what are words? Trying to grow a fruit tree in the wilderness.

"Go son, with my blessings. I give you nothing. And when you remember what I am saying you will come back. The land is still yours. As long as I am alive you will find a home waiting for you."

"Thank you, father."

"Before you go, see Chiremba. You are going out into the world. You need something to strengthen yourself. Tell him I shall pay him. Have a good journey, son."

"Thank you, father."

Nhamo smiled and felt a great love for his father. But there were things that belonged to his old world that were just lots of humbug on the mind, empty load, useless scrap. He would go to Chiremba but he would burn the charms as soon as he was away from home and its sickening environment. A man stands on his feet and guts. Charms were for you—so was God, though much later. But for us now the world is godless, no charms will work. All that is just the opium you take in the dark in the hope of a light. You don't need that now. You strike a match for a light. Nhamo laughed.

He could be so easily light-hearted. Now his brain worked with a fury only known to visionaries. The psychological ties were now broken, only the biological tied him to his father. He was free. He too remembered the aeroplane which his father had seen just before their talk. Space had no bounds and no ties. Floating laws ruled the darkness and he would float with the fiery balls. He was the sun, burning itself out every second and shedding tons of energy which it held in its power, giving it the thrust to drag its brood wherever it wanted to. This was the law that held him. The mystery that his father and ancestors had failed to grasp and which had caused their being wiped off the face of the earth. This thinking reached such a pitch that he began to sing, imitating as intimately as he could Satchmo's voice: "What a wonderful world." It was Satchmo's voice that he turned to when he felt buoyant.

Old Musoni did not look at his son as he left him. Already, his mind was trying to focus at some point in the dark unforeseeable future. Many things could happen and while he still breathed he would see that nothing terribly painful happened to his family, especially to his stubborn last born, Nhamo. Tomorrow, before sunrise, he would go to see Chiremba and ask him to throw bones over the future of his son. And if there were a couple of ancestors who needed appeasement, he would do it while he was still around.

He noticed that the sun was going down and he scraped the earth off his hoe.

The sun was sinking slowly, bloody red, blunting and blurring all the objects that had looked sharp in the light of day. Soon a chilly wind would blow over the land and the cold cloudless sky would send down beads of frost like white ants over the unprotected land.

Little Saigon

David St. John

Departure

I had been dreaming of
An albino peacock
Strutting before me along
The sun-washed hallways
Of my school, the best
School in all of Saigon
The nuns had told my
Shy Mother as they chatted
In French that first day.
A *lovely girl,* they cooed
To Mother as they stroked
The length of my braid.
That day, I looked out of
The tall scrubbed windows
Of the office & saw it,
White as ash . . . & in my dream
The sky itself unfolded
As the peacock
Slowly turned to face me,
Just the two of us alone,
& as it spread the fan

Of its tail I could see
Each elegant pale feather
Quietly catch flame . . .
Each feather burning like
The sails of the paper boats
We'd set adrift on the pond
Of the pavilion after
My Father died, a Buddhist
Farewell to the departed.
In my dream, the peacock
Flamed steadily to ash,
Then blew silently away,
Floating along the sudden
Gesture of a summer's breeze,
& I started shaking & crying,
No . . . it was my Mother
Shaking me, crying, as she
Whispered in my ear
So as not to wake my sister,
Ngoc Be, it's time! For weeks,
In secret, she'd met
With an old man who lived by
The tobacco shop, who knew
A Jack Pirate who'd take us
& the others on his boat, away
From this place, the new police
& the old police, the murders
Of our neighbors, Mother's
Friends . . . That night,
She handed me the suitcase
She'd already packed for
My sister Mai Chi and me,

& picking up my sister with
One arm & her own bag
With the other, she led us out
Of our sullen, damp apartment
Into the maze of alleys & lanes
Of our district, towards
The waterfront & the boat we'd
Leave on forever, forever
Towards a sunrise
Spreading pale & milky as
The peacock's quivering tail
At the horizon, towards some
Place of promises as distant
As any new world.

Adrift

The man who took our money
Pushed my Mother onto the other
Boat. Ours was too crowded
Already, he said, just room
For the two girls now. He
Was grinning. When Mai Chi saw
His black tongue and missing
Teeth, she began to cry. Mother
Was waving to us from the boat
Beside ours, her boat filling
With more like us, scared
& hopeful. We stood so close
Against the metal rail
As she yelled over to us, *Ngoc Be,
Mai Chi, don't be afraid . . .*

And as the two boats
Moved out from the cove in
The deep black of that midnight,
Mai Chi and I crouched there by
The rail even as the waves crashed
Up around us. The Jack Pirate
Captain, paid off by
All of us, started drinking right
There, even before the lights
Of the patrol towers disappeared.
We hated him and he hated us.
Days and days. And by the twentieth
Morning the only food and water
Still left were his, locked
In the trunk at the back of the boat,
& we were still nowhere, nowhere.
Your sister, my Mother had called
Out, *Take care of your sister* . . .
And when we both began to starve,
When Mai Chi's tongue swelled
Against her lips, her face
Peeling and cracked with a film
Of salt, I saw the Captain looking
At me, grinning at me. Even
At fourteen, I knew what
He wanted. *Give me water for my*
Sister, and food, I said. Then
He made me turn and face the waves,
My arms hooked over the metal rail.
Your sister's ugly like an animal,
He whispered, laughing, as he
Moved up against me from behind,

Pushing his hands and body up between
My legs as the waves below me
Waved to no one. For food, for water,
This is what happened to me for
Ten more nights, as we
Drifted, many of the men and women
Of our boat already collapsed along
Its filthy bottom, and dying,
Their children sprawled on top
Of them, none of them even lifting
Their heads to watch him as he'd
Push me against the side
Of the boat, as I faced the sea
And the stars splattered over
The blackness above and beneath me.
When the Australian fishing boat
Suddenly moved alongside us one
Morning, I was barely aware;
It was like a huge sunrise up close.
The fishermen carried us all
Onto their ship, giving us blankets,
Clean clothes, towels for the shower!
Then I saw two of the sailors from
The fishing boat lock the Jack Pirate's
Arms behind him, leading him off
As he yelled at them. I touched
Mai Chi on the top
Of her head. Then it was my turn
At last for the shower; for
The first time in weeks, I could
Wash the long streaks of dry blood
Off the inside of my thighs.

Little Saigon

At home in my French class
At school, the nuns made us skip
The chapter of our book called
La Vie Exotique de Hollywood!
But I read it anyway. A young
Parisian girl and her Uncle
Go and visit all the movie stars.
Now, here I am in California
And anyone who passes by
On the freeway to Long Beach
Can see the sign pointing the way
To Little Saigon, where we live now,
Mai Chi and I, with my Mother's
Cousin's family . . . even though
We wait each day for some news
Of our Mother, that she
Has finally arrived at a processing
Camp, that someone reliable has
Seen her, or the last, most
Horrible news we will not believe . . .
Even now, after three years,
Because time means nothing
When hope . . . I dream of her
Some nights, still adrift,
The only one still living, waving
To me in the blackness, saying
Ngoc Be, Mai Chi . . . I am coming . . .
Someday. But I know my Mother's
Cousin is ashamed of us,

Perhaps because she still believes
It was I who stood over the Jack Pirate
When his guard fell asleep one
Night, that it was I who carefully
Pushed the whole weight of
Her body onto the kitchen knife
Placed at the exact hollow
Of his windpipe. Perhaps.
Or maybe the shame is that I am
Now a young woman who bares her belly
To this extraordinary sunlight,
Immodestly my Mother's cousin
No doubt feels, so clearly &
Defiantly letting my nipples push
Through the blue velvet of my new
Halter top. *The shame, the shame . . .*
But I believe the real reason
Is because Mai Chi has finally
Come to look just like her Father,
The man who came sometimes
To stay with Mother and me
After my own Father had died—
A black American soldier who touched
My mother with such tenderness
None of her cousins would understand,
Nor ever admit to, here;
The beautiful black American man
Who hoisted me up onto his shoulders
And carried me along the paths
Of the gardens all during
That springtime, as jasmine bloomed.
My sister's Father, who she now

Resembles, the beautiful man
She's grown so closely to resemble,
Her skin shining deeply and dark,
Her hair black waves along her face
As we walk these streets
Of the familiar hateful neighborhood,
Mai Chi's small arm hooked into mine,
As we hold our heads up in the crowns
Of sunlight, regal as lost queens,
Making all the long-bitter & spiteful
Cousins of Little Saigon
Turn their terrible blank faces away.

My Parisian Aunt

Mother's cousin said to me
One night as I went out to meet
My friends, *If you're going*
To wear that spangly dress
You'll end up a whore
Just like your Aunt Kahnh in Paris!
Well, of course I was thrilled
& intrigued because I'd
Only known the few stories
My Mother had told of how
Her own sister had moved to Paris
As a young girl at the beginning
Of the war, leaving with an elegant
Older Frenchman who'd promised
To provide for her education
As well as an introduction to society.
Even though my Mother had only

Received one letter from Aunt
Kahnh in all those years,
She became a mythical presence
In our house, an emblem
Of some possible escape, a triumph
That we'd talk about over meals,
Imagining what she must be doing at
That very moment, the clothes
She was wearing, the leaves of the trees
In the famous parks falling
So exquisitely all around Kahnh
As she strolled on the arm of
Her noble protector. Her name
Grew to be a magical name in our house,
The lovely Kahnh who left for the world,
Who had all of Paris at her feet, who
Was the one that got away, as the men
Of our district told to each other
With noticeable regret. When
The blue letter arrived, announcing
Aunt Kahnh would soon visit,
My Mother's cousin wailed & wept,
Hissing over the boiling soup, *Whores*
In my house! And I remembered how
Mother told me once, *Ngoc Be,*
The only rule is to survive . . .
At last, the day we'd waited for—
Mai Chi's small hands shaking
Nervously, my own mouth
Dry with empty words. Aunt Kahnh
Stepped through the door
& placed gift

After gift into the thin open
Arms of Mother's cousin, who tried
Not to show her pleasure at
The long silk scarves
& tiny perfumes. Aunt Kahnh took
Mai Chi & me into the bedroom,
Softly, so softly
Closing the door behind her. She
Sat on the bed by us & took our
Hands into her own. She looked
So much like Mother then,
The tears gathering in her eyes,
Black strands of fine hair
Sticking to her cheeks, that
Mai Chi & I began to cry with her.
We leaned against her body,
Her smell of exotic flowers filling
The small room. *Ngoc Be*, she said,
Mai Chi . . . I want to take you back
With me to Paris; would you
Like that? Well, then
We started crying more, nodding
Yes, yes! & when I asked, *Why,*
Why now? Aunt Kahnh barely whispered
As she looked at us & said, *Ngoc Be,*
Mai Chi . . . your Mother is dead.

The Marais

How strange it was to speak
In French again, though I suppose
The old lessons of the nuns

Have served me well. We live in an
Ancient house that I love, here,
In the district called the Marais.
On the ground floor,
Aunt Kahnh's husband Eugene
Has his business, like his Father,
Selling elegant & elaborate picture
Frames, or making them especially
To order for museums & painters
All over the world! I love watching
The workers sculpt & chisel the wood,
Or lay out the fragile sheets
Of gilt. Sometimes, Eugene lets me
Have coffee with the painters,
Some very famous men & some no one
Has ever heard of—like
The handsome one who last week
Brought me some scraps of canvas
For the set of new paints
Aunt Kahnh has given me. I don't let
Anyone see my paintings though,
That is, anyone except
Mai Chi, of course. Eugene is good
To us, & even if Aunt Kahnh
Did not love him the way she does,
I would love him, though I do not believe
I have ever seen a man with so much
Silver hair, or a man who could drink
So much red wine with his dinner!
—That night, the night before
We left Little Saigon for good,
Aunt Kahnh told us that Mother did

Not suffer; Kahnh knew, she said,
Because a woman she trusted
Had been there, on the same boat,
When the storm came washing Mother
Overboard . . . her hand showing
Once above the waves, then
Nothing, that quickly & she was gone . . .
That's what the woman told Aunt Kahnh.
Last week, one night I stayed
So long upstairs painting that Mai Chi
Was sent up to bring me down for supper.
I had been working all day on my
New secret painting, but I showed it
To Mai Chi. It was of
Mother walking in old Saigon,
The beautiful streets of our childhood,
& beside her . . . the white peacock, its
Tail spread like a snow storm along
The whole of the background horizon.
When she saw it, Mai Chi began to
Shake, then cry. *When I dream*
Of Mother, Mai Chi said, *I see her like*
This, the peacock at her side.
Walking quietly at home . . .
I held Mai Chi & we both stared at
The painting. *Yes*, I said, *Mother is*
Telling us that she is finally safe . . .
We stood there together saying nothing
Until Mai Chi looked up at me
At last &
Said slowly, *Ngoc Be! So are we . . .*

Zelzah: A Tale From Long Ago

Norma Fox Mazer

Her name was Zelzah. It meant Shade-in-the-Heat. She was the second oldest of five daughters. Before her came Ruth; after her, Shulamith, Anna, and Sarah. Zelzah, quiet, often wondered about the names her mother had given her and her sisters. Anna, for instance, whose name meant "grace," was clumsy, with one leg shorter than the other. "Cripple, cripple, drown and dripple," other children chanted at her as she limped and hopped in the dusty street outside their house. As for Shulamith, it seemed sometimes that she lived only to do everything possible to disprove the meaning of her name, which was "peacefulness."

Shulamith went into a rage at the smallest detail. She insisted on fairness: the potato kugel must be cut into five equal portions for the sisters; a hair ribbon for Sarah must be shared with Anna; a letter from Aunt Hannah in America must be read aloud to everyone, or no one could hear it. "I insist," Shulamith cried. "I insist on fairness!"

The five sisters slept together in a large double bed. Although Ruth ("friendship"), who was wrong in the head, was the oldest, Shulamith dictated where each sister should sleep, and who would share what quilts. Anna and

Sarah, the youngest, slept across the bottom of the bed, head to toe, reversing sides every night so that neither got poked too often by their elder sisters' feet. Zelzah slept sandwiched between Ruth and Shulamith. All night, Ruth, who never said much during the day, only smiled at everyone and everything, groaned and muttered in her sleep, while Shulamith flung her arms around and turned a dozen times from side to side. Between these two, and with the little girls defenseless at her feet, Zelzah learned to sleep without moving, lying still on her back, her hands crossed over her belly.

Still, she was only human and there were occasions when her leg or her arm slipped over the invisible boundary into Shulamith's territory. At once, Shulamith screamed with fury. "Off my side, off, off!"

"Shulamith, Shulamith, peace, peace," Zelzah's mother would say in despairing tones. The mother was a small woman: small-boned, small hands, small feet; she had once been a beauty. After five miscarriages and five live births, her beauty had faded: she had the worn soft look of a piece of good linen that has been washed innumerable times. She had lived all her life in poverty and was an incurable optimist. Although her own name, Adah, meant ornament, and her whole life had been nothing but toil, she had still given each of her daughters a name she believed would help write her future.

"You are meant to be a comfort to those around you," she told Zelzah. "To your family now, to your husband and children someday. How wonderful it is to get out of the heat of summer into the shade! Just so, will your husband and children come to you for relief from strife and difficulties."

Zelzah loved this tiny mother who insisted against all evidence that names were destiny, and she tried very hard to live up to her name. She wanted to be a cool refreshing person, but summer or winter, her head sweated like a pig, her hands and feet were always red and burning, and in moments of stress she would be struck dumb. Thus, when Shulamith screamed at her in bed, "Off my side! Off, off, off!" Zelzah was helpless to calm her sister.

The bed the girls slept in stood in a corner of the one large whitewashed room that was their house. Besides the bed with its scrolled wooden headboard, the room contained a high dish cupboard, two wooden wardrobes, a scrubbed wooden table and chairs, several metal trunks with rounded tops and leather straps, a stove, and their parents' bed.

Each one of the girls had been born in that bed, each one had slept there for three or four years with her parents before moving into the bed with her sisters, to make room for the new baby.

Their father, Jacob, worked on leather; he was a tanner. He dragged himself home each night smelling horribly. His hands were permanently stained the color of old boots. Sometimes their mother wanted to sleep with the girls, but where could they find room for another body? They lived in Poland, they were Jewish, and all this was a good many years ago.

Of course they were poor. All the Jews in the little village of Premzl were poor. In Warsaw, they heard, there were wealthy Jews, Jews with servants, even, but here in Premzl goats were tethered by the houses, and chickens pecked in the streets.

Stories of America, the golden land, whistled between

the houses like the wind. At night, Zelzah's parents whispered in their bed. Zelzah's mother sewed a pocket into the bottom of her mattress, and there, whenever she could, she put aside a bit of money. In the winter on market days she rose before dawn to bake rolls. She wrapped them in napkins, carried them to the marketplace, and sold them, singing, "Hot rolls, hot hot hot, hot rolls." Under her skirt she kept a hot brick to warm her chilled feet and legs.

The girls, too, did whatever they could. Anna, the cripple, ran errands for the neighbors, her shoulders listing, accepting the coins she was given with a sullen smile. Ruth would do whatever task she was set to in the house. If no one told her to sweep the floor, or stir the washing in the tub on the stove, she would pick up a stick, a bug, a crushed leaf, and bringing it close to her eyes, stare at it for hours. Shulamith and Zelzah did a bit of everything. Only Sarah, the youngest ("princess"), was petted and allowed to play all day.

At the age of nine, Zelzah went to work on the farm of an elderly Polish couple. The woman's fingers were bent like claws and she could no longer feed the chickens, do her housework, baking, and all the other things that had to be done on a farm. Zelzah took over these tasks. It was hard work, but she was well fed, and was often outdoors. She worked for the couple for six years, uncomplaining, walking three miles each way every day. Her hands were coarse and red. Her body became sturdy, and her arms were strong.

Her parents began to speak of her future. They wanted a good husband for their Zelzah. They discussed this boy, that boy, another one. Ruth, though older, would of course stay home with them. Zelzah would be the first of the sisters to marry. Zelzah listened, sometimes smiling, cracking her reddened knuckles, saying little. Then, on the farm, standing outside the cow's stall, for instance, her feet planted squarely in the mucky yard, holding a bucket of fresh warm milk, the flies thick on the rim, some already drowned in the milk, she would lift her face and squint into the distance. Strange thoughts went through her mind. A wind might be blowing gently. Or the sun shining. Goldfinches dipped across the fields. Life seemed wonderful, although she didn't know why and would never have said it aloud. The thought of marriage made her sigh over and over.

"I want to get married," Shulamith whispered fiercely into Zelzah's ear at night. "Why did Mama have you before me? I want to have my own bed and sleep in it with a man!"

Zelzah snorted behind her hand. Shulamith tickled her suddenly, and Zelzah thrashed around, shrieking with laughter.

Later that summer, a letter from Aunt Hannah came from America, from a town named Stratton in a place called Vermont. Aunt Hannah had four sons, "all good, kind boys, and smart, too," she wrote. One was already married to an American girl. One was still young. Two sons, Jake and Ephraim, needed wives. Aunt Hannah thought Zelzah, now fifteen, would make a good wife for her son Jake. She would pay half Zelzah's boat fare.

Zelzah's mother counted her little hoard of money. There was enough for half a boat fare plus a little extra to give Zelzah wrapped in a handkerchief, which was then tucked carefully into the wicker case with leather straps that held her clothing.

Cold winds blew in the village when Zelzah left. The boat would be cold. She wore a gray wool blouse, a long black worsted skirt, a heavy coat that had been her father's and that smelled like a tannery, a scarf on her head, and a wool shawl over her shoulders. The shawl, gray, with black fringe, was her mother's. On the boat, Zelzah wept into the fringe. She was not seasick; she endured without complaint the crowding, the stifling odors, the groans, noises, and cries of the hundreds of people with whom she was packed into steerage; once every day she ate bread and a bit of hard dry cheese with good appetite. Yet, for the forty-two days of the voyage, tears poured steadily from her eyes.

Aunt Hannah met her at the dock in New York City. Thank God, Aunt Hannah looked like Zelzah's mother, her very own sister! How else would Zelzah have known that this was, indeed, her aunt, and not just one of the hundreds of women milling around?

Aunt Hannah hugged Zelzah. She was small, like Zelzah's mother, with the same bright black eyes, but with prematurely white hair. And her cheeks, unlike her sister's, were bright, blooming. She pinched Zelzah's cheek and said in Yiddish, "You're a fine, strong-looking girl. Tell me how my sister is, tell me everything!"

"Yes, they're fine, all fine," Zelzah said, looking around. The noise made her ears ache. She longed to close her eyes against the swarms of people, carts, horses, buildings, signs, wagons, dogs, and God knew what else! It had really happened, then! She had left home, crossed the ocean, come to America. Remembering the tears she had wept on the voyage, her eyes ached as if to shed more tears. She stuffed the fringes of her shawl into her mouth and followed Aunt Hannah.

They took a train to Vermont, and from the station walked two miles to the village. It was night. There was snow everywhere in great dazzling white drifts. The stars were icy in the dark sky. Zelzah walked beside Aunt Hannah, her breath blowing out before her in a white cloud. Her wicker case bumped against her leg, the snow crunched beneath her feet. Aunt Hannah told her about the small grocery store she and Uncle Morris owned in Stratton. In Zelzah's honor, Aunt Hannah said, the store was closed early.

They came to a wooden building, two stories high. Aunt Hannah led the way up a dim, narrow flight of stairs. "Here we are, dear child!"

Zelzah was trembling. Her legs felt weak. There was a blur of male faces and voices. Uncle Morris, a short sweaty man with tight gray curls, embraced her, his long soft mustache brushing her face. His eyes were kind. Her cousins were introduced, one, two, three, Jake, Ephraim, Sammy. Michel, the oldest, was married and had gone west with his bride. All this Zelzah heard as if from a distance. Her stomach rocked as if now, off the boat, she was for the first time seasick.

"Sit down, sit down." Uncle Morris pushed her into a large overstuffed chair. "Hannah, bring some wine. Ephraim, here, take your cousin's case." But Zelzah wouldn't release her grip on the wicker case.

The room she was in was crowded with furniture: couches, a dark oak sideboard on top of which trays, glasses, bottles, and framed pictures bumped against one another, many little tables with kerosene lamps, ashtrays, a piano, and a large gate-leg table overflowing with books and papers. Small woven rugs were scattered around on the carpeted floor, and thick red velvet curtains, their tassels sweeping the floor, covered the windows. Zelzah's head spun, her ears were burning, her head sweating. With moist burning hands, she clutched the wicker case, nodding and bobbing her head.

Downstairs, behind the store, there was still another room; here, Aunt Hannah had made a place for Zelzah. She had laid a colorful little rag rug on the wooden floor, and the rocking chair had a bright red cushion. A calendar hung on a nail, showing a picture of a deer fleeing into snow-covered woods. The date of Zelzah's arrival was circled. There was a bed, and a marble-topped bureau with three drawers and a special place for the white chamber pot that had a bunch of daisies painted on the side.

"You're so kind, so very kind, too kind," Zelzah said. It was very cold; the windows were iced with frost flowers. Zelzah stared shyly at the iron cot with its single mattress covered by a gray wool blanket. Imagine. A bed just for her.

After Aunt Hannah left, Zelzah sat on the edge of the bed, staring down at her heavy black shoes. How handsome Cousin Ephraim was! There was something dashing and bold about him, about his bold eyes and thick black mustache. His eyes had danced over her as he greeted her in English. When she stammered something in Yiddish, he had laughed and pinched her cheek as if she were so much younger than he. Then he had turned to his mother and said something quickly, again in English, which had made Aunt Hannah laugh and swat his hands lightly. Zelzah was glad he was not the one Aunt Hannah wanted her for.

As for Jake, she had only peeked at him, keeping her scarf over her head and drawn almost down to her eyes, out of fear and shyness. "How do you do, dear cousin, are you tired from the trip?" he had said. Such kind words. Jake wasn't handsome like Ephraim, but—beautiful! She had never seen a man so beautiful. His eyes were as blue as the sky over the Polish farm on a summer day, his nose was long and fine, his mouth full, soft, gentle. He wore soft leather boots, and the hand that pressed hers in greeting was dry and warm. "Ah," she sighed, astonished by his beauty.

Each morning of her new life, Zelzah woke before dawn, as she always had, dressed hurriedly in the frigid room, used the outside "facilities," and joined the family for breakfast. Sammy went each day to school, Ephraim to work in an office, Jake to work in the paper mill, while Zelzah joined Uncle Morris and Aunt Hannah in the store. On the first day, speaking kindly but firmly, Aunt Hannah said, "Now, Zelzah, no more Yiddish. You must learn to speak like an American."

Through the winter and into the spring, she worked in the store. At first she hardly dared speak, but little by little she learned American phrases, American money, and American behavior. She gave up wearing her shawl in public, and did her best not to embarrass the family.

At night, though, she still slept with the shawl next to her face and often wept into its fringes. She thought of her sisters, and especially of Shulamith. How quiet these sons of Aunt Hannah were! She couldn't get accustomed to sleeping alone in a bed, to being all alone through the night in a room with not another soul in it.

Often she lay awake for hours, staring into the dark, straining to hear—something. A sigh, a groan, a cough, the whispers of her parents as they lay together. Outside, dogs barked. Or an owl hooted. Far away, a horse might whinny.

The night was no darker than all the other nights of her life had been, but she lay awake, her heart swollen with terror and loneliness.

Yet everyone was kind to her. Uncle Morris gave her chocolates and patted her head reassuringly when she made mistakes. Ephraim teased that he was getting tired of these American girls who couldn't stay away from him, and said, laughingly, "Watch out, brother Jake!" Aunt Hannah was pleased with every American word Zelzah learned and praised the immaculate way she kept her room and her person.

Her young cousin, Sammy, sometimes showed her his schoolbooks, pointing out a word here and there. As for Jake, he spoke to her gravely, asking her questions about her sisters, the work she had done on the farm, the village where she had lived. He listened to everything she said, his eyes melancholy. She wondered what made him sad. When she lapsed into Yiddish, he shook his head reproachfully. "Speak English, Zelzah. Yiddish is for greenies." He spent most of his time reading books. Zelzah had never read a whole book. In the summer, they were to be married.

The weather was still cold, although winter had retreated, when Jake came to Zelzah's room one night. He got into her bed. His bony legs and feet were icy. Zelzah held him close, warming him. He came to her bed one or two nights every week. After his visits, Zelzah always slept more soundly. She thought Jake's eyes were not so sad anymore. As he lay in her arms, she whispered to him in Yiddish, "I would like a cat when we have our own home." She had never asked anyone for anything; it struck her that she was becoming brave, even American. She rubbed her hands in Jake's hair. He smelled good, like fresh-baked bread. He was always cold, and she was always warm, burning, her head steaming: She thought of her name, Shade-in-the-Heat; was not warmth in winter just as good?

In spring, Ephraim, who had many girlfriends, brought home a new girl to meet his mother. Her name was Grace. She was a college student and spoke quickly, laughing often. "How do you do!" she said to Zelzah, holding out her hand and then shaking Zelzah's hand forcefully. She was a tall girl with long hands and feet. "So you're reading Dickens," she said to Jake. "He's out of fashion, but I think he's wonderful, don't you?"

The next time Grace came to the house, she and Jake and Ephraim all went out for a walk in the fresh evening. Zelzah was glad they didn't ask her. She felt shy and ignorant around Grace. Soon, Grace began to drop in on her own, often when Ephraim wasn't around. She and Jake argued furiously about books and politics. Then, for a while, she stopped coming to the house. And Jake stopped coming to Zelzah's room at night.

Well, well, Zelzah said to herself several months later, it's not surprising. No, not surprising. She seemed to be quite calm. She listened calmly as Aunt Hannah, weeping and hugging her, said that Grace was pregnant, that in fact Grace and Jake had been secretly married for some time.

They were in Zelzah's little room behind the store, sitting on the iron cot with its neatly laid blanket. "Oh, what a disgrace, I'm so ashamed," Aunt Hannah said, looking at Zelzah with reddened eyes. She seized Zelzah's hands. "And I promised my sister—" Fresh tears threatened. She drew Zelzah's hands to her heart. "Dear child! Do you want to stay on? You're always welcome. But they are going to live here. Grace and Jake. Until the baby is born, at least. Oh, what will you do now?"

"I will think of something," Zelzah said, in Yiddish. She felt a little cold and hunched her shoulders, drawing her mother's shawl closer around herself.

It was now fall again, nearly a year since Zelzah had come to America. Uncle Morris and Aunt Hannah went with her to the train station. She carried her wicker case and a bag of fruit and sandwiches Aunt Hannah had made for her. "You can always come back," Aunt Hannah said. "If you need us, we're here, right here!"

Uncle Morris pressed a chunk of white chocolate and then a five-dollar bill into her hands. Zelzah boarded the train, took a seat, and put her wicker case at her feet. Her hands were sticky with chocolate. She put the chocolate down on the seat, tucked the money into the little leather purse Aunt Hannah had given her, and wiped her hands on her handkerchief. The train jerked and puffed. She looked out the cinder-specked window. Aunt Hannah and Uncle Morris were waving, moving alongside the train as it slowly left the station.

"Good-bye, good-bye," Zelzah said. Her eyes were moist, but suddenly she wanted to laugh. A wind seemed to blow through her, and she recalled the blue Polish sky and goldfinches bobbing over the fields. She drew the handkerchief to her mouth so that Aunt Hannah and Uncle Morris wouldn't see her laughing. The train picked up speed.

In New York City she found her way to a family whom Aunt Hannah had recommended. Here she was given a bed and meals for a small sum. She found work almost at once in a dress factory situated in a loft. All winter she sat at a sewing machine for nine hours a day, six days a week. She made $11 a week. She was nearly seventeen years old.

Work in the factory was hard; the loft was boiling in the summer, freezing in the winter. But Zelzah was strong. Two nights a week she went to school to learn to read and write English. Every month she sent money to her family; Shulamith was planning to come to America to join Zelzah.

In spring Zelzah heard from Aunt Hannah that Grace had died in childbirth. She remembered Grace saying, "I think Dickens is wonderful!" She sat up for many hours that night thinking about her life, thinking of Jake with his cold feet and bony legs. Now he had an infant girl, but no wife to care for the child or him. Zelzah had begun to see that there were things she might like to do in the world. She had left her village in Poland, traveled across Europe, then the Atlantic Ocean. She had gone from New York to Vermont, and back to New York. Now she knew there were other places to go, and she thought that she would no longer be afraid to go to them. Pennsylvania! Wisconsin! North Carolina! South Dakota! The names rang like bells in her head. She was reading the newspapers now, and sometimes a book. She had bought herself a few new clothes, a coat, shoes, a muff for her hands on bitter mornings.

She thought of all this, of the money she sent home, of the hope of Shulamith joining her. And then of her mother telling her the meaning of her name, the meaning of her life.

After this, she wrote a letter in English, being careful to spell each word properly. "My Dear Cousin Jake, I have heard recently of your Tragic News. I send you my

Heartfelt Sympathy. There are tears in my Heart, for you. I want to say something in Plain Words. Would you need me now to be your wife? If that is the Truth, I will be happy to oblige." (She crossed out "to oblige.") "Kiss the dear little baby Girl for me. Zelzah."

And Jake answered, "Zelzah, dear cousin, my heart is too full of grief to consider this matter now. My mother takes care of the child, and I am going to Michigan to see if I can obtain the college education I so deeply desire, and which my beloved wife (whom I will mourn forever) believed I ought to have. Your cousin, in friendship, Jake Neuborg."

Reading Jake's letter, again that impulse to laugh overcame Zelzah. Although there was no one to see her, she stuffed her fingers into her mouth, stifling the laughter. She didn't understand herself. Was this a laughing matter!

Several years passed. At last Shulamith came to America. She wore high black boots and looked around her, scowling ferociously. "This noise, this noise!" She clapped her hands to her ears.

"You'll get used to it," Zelzah said, calmly. Passing through the throngs of people, gripping her sister firmly by the elbow, Zelzah caught sight of herself in a store window. She had changed. It was the first thing Shulamith had said. "Zelzah, is it you?" She had cut her hair; then, working and studying without much rest, eating less so she could send money home—these things had honed her down. She no longer had plump, bright-red cheeks. She was surprised, even a little alarmed to see herself; then she smiled.

Shulamith went to work in the same dress factory as Zelzah, but at once she hated it. She raged against it every day. "I'm getting out of here, I won't go on for years like you, Zelzah. Don't you ever get angry? Look at you, smiling, and you were jilted by our cousin. If a man ever did that to me!"

At night, she shoved Zelzah in the bed they shared. "Move! Move! You're on my side." Often, Zelzah got out of bed and read into the middle of the night, the fringed shawl over her shoulders.

In the morning, Shulamith was always up first. She prepared breakfast for the two of them. Sometimes she sang, but when the factory came into sight, she broke off, scowling, and raised her fist to the ugly building. She began night school also, but was not in the same class as Zelzah.

Zelzah was now hoping to get a high school diploma. She was studying mathematics, history, and geography. When she and Shulamith walked to school, they linked arms, and Shulamith spoke of their parents and sisters, answering Zelzah's questions.

On warm Sundays, they often took the trolley to Brooklyn to walk in the woods, picking mushrooms or bunches of soft floppy little violets. One day, coming upon a farm, they sat on a bench and were given mugs of thick yellow milk.

"I used to milk cows," Zelzah said.

"You!" The farm woman smiled disbelievingly. "You!"

Linking hands, suddenly, like two children, Zelzah and Shulamith danced around, shouting with laughter. And the farm woman laughed, too, seeing that she was right and Zelzah, the young lady from the city, had only been teasing.

On one of these Sunday expeditions, Shulamith met a "landsman," a red-haired young man from a village near Premzl. The first time he came to visit them, Shulamith left the room, leaving Aaron and Zelzah together.

"Don't do that again," Zelzah said that night when she and Shulamith were alone, getting ready for bed. Shulamith, frowning, brushed her hair over her face.

"And why not? He can come to see you as well as me!"

"Listen, my dear child," Zelzah said, as if she were years older than Shulamith, rather than only ten months. "I have no interest in the young man."

"But you're older," Shulamith said, brushing her hair furiously. "It's only fair! I want you to be happy!"

"Peace, Shulamith, peace," Zelzah said, just as their mother had done so many years ago.

Aaron was a locksmith; a good trade. Shulamith's rages left him undismayed; he had an even temperament and thought her quite wonderful. A year after they met, they were married. Shulamith insisted that the wedding pictures include Zelzah.

As the three of them stood outside Temple Beth Israel with their arms around each other, free hands holding down their hats against the warm gusts of May wind, Zelzah thought of the last letter she had received from her mother. "I long to see my dear Zelzah, my dear Shade-in-the-Heat. Send me good news soon! If I cannot see you, then the news of your happiness will satisfy me." Anna had been married the previous spring; Sarah was engaged. Only Ruth, who still stared for hours with dreamy satisfaction at a stick of wood (or so Shulamith had told her), and Zelzah were still unmarried.

The next year when Shulamith had her first child, Zelzah received her high school diploma. She left the factory and went to work in an office. Not more money, but far less strenuous work. Her eyes had been going bad in the factory; now she had to wear glasses for reading and close work. "So?" Shulamith said, when Zelzah visited to give her the good news of her new job. "Will you settle down now?"

Zelzah started college classes at night. For eleven years she went to college. For eleven years, each time she had an exam, she found it impossible to sleep and sat up all night with the gray fringed shawl over her shoulders, feverishly muttering dates, names, places, and formulas to herself. Only once did she fail an exam, in physics; that was the year when two days before the exam Shulamith had her third child and nearly died.

After she received her bachelor's degree, Zelzah was offered a job teaching third grade in a medium-sized city in upstate New York. There she rented a three-room apartment in a private home. The house was painted a fresh yellow on the outside, and had a large porch running around three sides. Zelzah had her own entrance, a tiny but efficient kitchen, and windows looking out on the back and side yards where the landlady, Mrs. Zimmerman, kept flowers and bushes blooming seven months of the year.

Every summer Zelzah visited Shulamith, Aaron, and their six children in the bungalow they rented in the Catskill Mountains. She stayed with them for a week or ten days, playing with the children, and talking to Shulamith for hours on end. She adored her nieces and nephews; she thought them all clever and beautiful, and she was always glad to leave the excitement and untidiness of their lives.

Thus, Zelzah's life. Her cats, interesting creatures. Her windows full of plants. A month of travel in the summer. Shulamith, Aaron, and the children. (She kept all their letters and notes in a little square metal candy box with blue flowers painted all over it.) And her third-grade students; often they returned years later to visit her, to tell her what they were doing, and how well they were doing it. She remembered all their names.

The winter of her fortieth birthday, Zelzah received a letter from Shulamith. "You could still get married," she wrote. "You are better-looking now than when you were younger. Come to visit us over the winter holidays, I want you to meet a friend. He was widowed six months ago. A lovely man! I want you to be happy!"

But Zelzah was involved with a pageant her third-grade children were writing and producing. There would be rehearsals over the vacation. The pageant was about the spirit of America and how the children's parents had come from so many different lands. Really, the children had done a lovely job! She wrote Shulamith her regrets. "Perhaps another time, I'll be able to come in the winter."

A few months later, she woke up one morning and thought how strange life was. It was 6 A.M. She had never shaken the habit of rising early. Zelzah had been dreaming about her sisters. She seemed to hear Shulamith shouting, "Move! It isn't fair!" She thought of the Polish farm, the dirty cows, herself a child dreaming with a bucket of warm milk in each hand. She thought of Jake pressing his cold body against hers. And of frost flowers on the window. Of the chocolates Uncle Morris had given her, and of drinking thick yellow milk in a farmyard. She thought of blue-covered examination books, the angry red faces of each one of Shulamith's babies, and then of the pink dress she had bought herself for spring.

Emma jumped on her stomach and began cleaning her paws. Zelzah pushed the cat to one side and, with her hands behind her head, did twenty sit-ups. She got out of bed and put her mother's shawl around her shoulders. She held the shawl to her face for a moment, then washed in cold water. Mother and father, both, were long dead. She made herself coffee, ate an orange and buttered toast. She thought of the day ahead of her, of the children she would teach. She set down her coffee cup and hastened to get dressed. She was humming under her breath, her mind was filled with details of the day ahead of her. Was she happy? Who could say? Zelzah, herself, never thought in such terms. What was happiness? Did anyone know?

"Recitatif"

Toni Morrison

My mother danced all night and Roberta's was sick. That's why we were taken to St. Bonny's. People want to put their arms around you when you tell them you were in a shelter, but it really wasn't bad. No big long room with one hundred beds like Bellevue. There were four to a room, and when Roberta and me came, there was a shortage of state kids, so we were the only ones assigned to 406 and could go from bed to bed if we wanted to. And we wanted to, too. We changed beds every night and for the whole four months we were there we never picked one out as our own permanent bed.

It didn't start out that way. The minute I walked in and the Big Bozo introduced us, I got sick to my stomach. It was one thing to be taken out of your own bed early in the morning—it was something else to be stuck in a strange place with a girl from a whole other race. And Mary, that's my mother, she was right. Every now and then she would stop dancing long enough to tell me something important and one of the things she said was that they never washed their hair and they smelled funny. Roberta sure did. Smell funny, I mean. So when the Big Bozo (nobody ever called her Mrs. Itkin, just like nobody ever said St. Bonaventure)— when she said, "Twyla, this is Roberta. Roberta, this is Twyla.

Make each other welcome," I said, "My mother won't like you putting me in here."

"Good," said Bozo. "Maybe then she'll come and take you home."

How's that for mean? If Roberta had laughed I would have killed her, but she didn't. She just walked over to the window and stood with her back to us.

"Turn around," said the Bozo. "Don't be rude. Now Twyla. Roberta. When you hear a loud buzzer, that's the call for dinner. Come down to the first floor. Any fights and no movie." And then, just to make sure we knew what we would be missing, "*The Wizard of Oz.*"

Roberta must have thought I meant that my mother would be mad about my being put in the shelter. Not about rooming with her, because as soon as Bozo left she came over to me and said, "Is your mother sick too?"

"No," I said. "She just likes to dance all night."

"Oh." She nodded her head and I liked the way she understood things so fast. So for the moment it didn't matter that we looked like salt and pepper standing there and that's what the other kids called us sometimes. We were eight years old and got F's all the time. Me because I couldn't remember what I read or what the teacher said. And Roberta because she couldn't read at all and didn't even listen to the teacher. She wasn't good at anything except jacks, at which she was a killer: pow scoop pow scoop pow scoop.

We didn't like each other all that much at first, but nobody else wanted to play with us because we weren't real orphans with beautiful dead parents in the sky. We were dumped. Even the New York City Puerto Ricans and the upstate Indians ignored us. All kinds of kids were in there, black ones, white ones, even two Koreans. The food was

good, though. At least I thought so. Roberta hated it and
left whole pieces of things on her plate: Spam, Salisbury
steak—even Jell-O with fruit cocktail in it, and she didn't
care if I ate what she wouldn't. Mary's idea of supper was
popcorn and a can of Yoo-Hoo. Hot mashed potatoes and
two weenies was like Thanksgiving for me.

It really wasn't bad, St. Bonny's. The big girls on the
second floor pushed us around now and then. But that was
all. They wore lipstick and eyebrow pencil and wobbled
their knees while they watched TV. Fifteen, sixteen, even,
some of them were. They were put-out girls, scared run-
aways most of them. Poor little girls who fought their
uncles off but looked tough to us, and mean. God, did they
look mean. The staff tried to keep them separate from the
younger children, but sometimes they caught us watching
them in the orchard where they played radios and danced
with each other. They'd light out after us and pull our hair
or twist our arms. We were scared of them, Roberta and me,
but neither of us wanted the other one to know it. So we
got a good list of dirty names we could shout back when we
ran from them through the orchard. I used to dream a lot
and almost always the orchard was there. Two acres, four
maybe, of these little apple trees. Hundreds of them. Empty
and crooked like beggar women when I first came to St.
Bonny's but fat with flowers when I left. I don't know why
I dreamt about that orchard so much. Nothing really happened there. Nothing all that important, I mean. Just the
big girls dancing and playing the radio. Roberta and me
watching. Maggie fell down there once. The kitchen
woman with legs like parentheses. And the big girls
laughed at her. We should have helped her up, I know, but
we were scared of those girls with lipstick and eyebrow
pencil. Maggie couldn't talk. The kids said she had her

tongue cut out, but I think she was just born that way: mute. She was old and sandy-colored and she worked in the kitchen. I don't know if she was nice or not. I just remember her legs like parentheses and how she rocked when she walked. She worked from early in the morning till two o'clock, and if she was late, if she had too much cleaning and didn't get out till two-fifteen or so, she'd cut through the orchard so she wouldn't miss her bus and have to wait another hour. She wore this really stupid little hat—a kid's hat with ear flaps—and she wasn't much taller than we were. A really awful little hat. Even for a mute, it was dumb—dressing like a kid and never saying anything at all.

"But what about if somebody tries to kill her?" I used to wonder about that. "Or what if she wants to cry? Can she cry?"

"Sure," Roberta said. "But just tears. No sounds come out."

"She can't scream?"

"Nope. Nothing."

"Can she hear?"

"I guess."

"Let's call her," I said. And we did.

"Dummy! Dummy!" She never turned her head.

"Bow legs! Bow legs!" Nothing. She just rocked on, the chin straps of her baby-boy hat swaying from side to side. I think we were wrong. I think she could hear and didn't let on. And it shames me even now to think there was somebody in there after all who heard us call her those names and couldn't tell on us.

We got along all right, Roberta and me. Changed beds every night, got F's in civics and communication skills and gym. The Bozo was disappointed in us, she said. Out of 130 of us state cases, 90 were under twelve. Almost all were real orphans with beautiful dead parents in the sky. We were the only ones dumped and the only ones with F's in three classes including gym. So we got along—what with her leaving whole pieces of things on her plate and being nice about not asking questions.

I think it was the day before Maggie fell down that we found out our mothers were coming to visit us on the same Sunday. We had been at the shelter twenty-eight days (Roberta twenty-eight and a half) and this was their first visit with us. Our mothers would come at ten o'clock in time for chapel, then lunch with us in the teachers' lounge. I thought if my dancing mother met her sick mother it might be good for her. And Roberta thought her sick mother would get a big bang out of a dancing one. We got excited about it and curled each other's hair. After breakfast we sat on the bed watching the road from the window. Roberta's socks were still wet. She washed them the night before and put them on the radiator to dry. They hadn't, but she put them on anyway because their tops were so pretty—scalloped in pink. Each of us had a purple construction-paper basket that we had made in craft class. Mine had a yellow crayon rabbit on it. Roberta's had eggs with wiggly lines of color. Inside were cellophane grass and just the jelly beans because I'd eaten the two marshmallow eggs they gave us. The Big Bozo came herself to get us. Smiling, she told us we looked very nice and to come downstairs. We were so surprised by the smile we'd never seen before, neither of us moved.

"Don't you want to see your mommies?"

I stood up first and spilled the jelly beans all over the floor. Bozo's smile disappeared while we scrambled to get the candy up off the floor and put it back in the grass.

She escorted us downstairs to the first floor, where the

other girls were lining up to file into the chapel. A bunch of grown-ups stood to one side. Viewers mostly. The old biddies who wanted servants and the fags who wanted company looking for children they might want to adopt. Once in a while a grandmother. Almost never anybody young or anybody whose face wouldn't scare you in the night. Because if any of the real orphans had young relatives they wouldn't be real orphans. I saw Mary right away. She had on those green slacks I hated and hated even more now because didn't she know we were going to chapel? And that fur jacket with the pocket linings so ripped she had to pull to get her hands out of them. But her face was pretty—like always—and she smiled and waved like she was the little girl looking for her mother, not me.

I walked slowly, trying not to drop the jelly beans and hoping the paper handle would hold. I had to use my last Chiclet because by the time I finished cutting everything out, all the Elmer's was gone. I am left-handed and the scissors never worked for me. It didn't matter, though; I might just as well have chewed the gum. Mary dropped to her knees and grabbed me, mashing the basket, the jelly beans, and the grass into her ratty fur jacket.

"Twyla, baby. Twyla, baby!"

I could have killed her. Already I heard the big girls in the orchard the next time saying, "Twyyyyyla, baby!" But I couldn't stay mad at Mary while she was smiling and hugging me and smelling of Lady Esther dusting powder. I wanted to stay buried in her fur all day.

To tell the truth I forgot about Roberta. Mary and I got in line for the traipse into chapel and I was feeling proud because she looked so beautiful even in those ugly green slacks that made her behind stick out. A pretty mother on earth is better than a beautiful dead one in the sky even if she did leave you all alone to go dancing.

I felt a tap on my shoulder, turned, and saw Roberta smiling. I smiled back, but not too much lest somebody think this visit was the biggest thing that ever happened in my life. Then Roberta said, "Mother, I want you to meet my roommate, Twyla. And that's Twyla's mother."

I looked up it seemed for miles. She was big. Bigger than any man and on her chest was the biggest cross I'd ever seen. I swear it was six inches long each way. And in the crook of her arm was the biggest Bible ever made.

Mary, simpleminded as ever, grinned and tried to yank her hand out of the pocket with the raggedy lining—to shake hands, I guess. Roberta's mother looked down at me and then looked down at Mary too. She didn't say anything, just grabbed Roberta with her Bible-free hand and stepped out of line, walking quickly to the rear of it. Mary was still grinning because she's not too swift when it comes to what's really going on. Then this light bulb goes off in her head and she says "That bitch!" really loud and us almost in the chapel now. Organ music whining; the Bonny Angels singing sweetly. Everybody in the world turned around to look. And Mary would have kept it up—kept calling names if I hadn't squeezed her hands as hard as I could. That helped a little, but she still twitched and crossed and uncrossed her legs all through service. Even groaned a couple of times. Why did I think she would come there and act right? Slacks. No hat like the grandmothers and viewers, and groaning all the while. When we stood for hymns she kept her mouth shut. Wouldn't even look at the words on the page. She actually reached in her purse for a mirror to check her lipstick. All I could think of was that she really needed to be killed. The sermon lasted a year, and I knew the real orphans were looking smug again.

We were supposed to have lunch in the teachers' lounge, but Mary didn't bring anything, so we picked fur and cellophane grass off the mashed jelly beans and ate them. I could have killed her. I sneaked a look at Roberta. Her mother had brought chicken legs and ham sandwiches and oranges and a whole box of chocolate-covered grahams. Roberta drank milk from a thermos while her mother read the Bible to her.

Things are not right. The wrong food is always with the wrong people. Maybe that's why I got into waitress work later—to match up the right people with the right food. Roberta just let those chicken legs sit there, but she did bring a stack of grahams up to me later when the visit was over. I think she was sorry that her mother would not shake my mother's hand. And I liked that and I liked the fact that she didn't say a word about Mary groaning all the way through the service and not bringing any lunch.

Roberta left in May when the apple trees were heavy and white. On her last day we went to the orchard to watch the big girls smoke and dance by the radio. It didn't matter that they said, "Twyyyyyla, baby." We sat on the ground and breathed. Lady Esther. Apple blossoms. I still go soft when I smell one or the other. Roberta was going home. The big cross and the big Bible was coming to get her and she seemed sort of glad and sort of not. I thought I would die in that room of four beds without her and I knew Bozo had plans to move some other dumped kid in there with me. Roberta promised to write every day, which was really sweet of her because she couldn't read a lick so how could she write anybody? I would have drawn pictures and sent them to her but she never gave me her address. Little by little she faded. Her wet socks with the

pink scalloped tops and her big serious-looking eyes—
that's all I could catch when I tried to bring her to mind.

I was working behind the counter at the Howard Johnson's
on the Thruway just before the Kingston exit. Not a bad
job. Kind of a long ride from Newburgh, but okay once I
got there. Mine was the second night shift, eleven to
seven. Very light until a Greyhound checked in for breakfast around six-thirty. At that hour the sun was all the way
clear of the hills behind the restaurant. The place looked
better at night—more like shelter—but I loved it when
the sun broke in, even if it did show all the cracks in the
vinyl and the speckled floor looked dirty no matter what
the mop boy did.

It was August and a bus crowd was just unloading. They
would stand around a long while: going to the john, and
looking at gifts and junk for sale machines, reluctant to sit
down so soon. Even to eat. I was trying to fill the coffee-
pots and get them all situated on the electric burners when
I saw her. She was sitting in a booth smoking a cigarette
with two guys smothered in head and facial hair. Her own
hair was so big and wild I could hardly see her face. But the
eyes. I would know them anywhere. She had on a powder-
blue halter and shorts outfit and earrings the size of brace-
lets. Talk about lipstick and eyebrow pencil. She made the
big girls look like nuns. I couldn't get off the counter until
seven o'clock, but I kept watching the booth in case they
got up to leave before that. My replacement was on time
for a change, so I counted and stacked my receipts as fast as
I could and signed off. I walked over to the booth, smiling
and wondering if she would remember me. Or even if she
wanted to remember me. Maybe she didn't want to be
reminded of St. Bonny's or to have anybody know she was

ever there. I know I never talked about it to anybody.

I put my hands in my apron pockets and leaned against the back of the booth facing them.

"Roberta? Roberta Fisk?"

She looked up. "Yeah?"

"Twyla."

She squinted for a second and then said, "Wow."

"Remember me?"

"Sure. Hey. Wow."

"It's been awhile," I said, and gave a smile to the two hairy guys.

"Yeah. Wow. You work here?"

"Yeah," I said. "I live in Newburgh."

"Newburgh? No kidding?" She laughed then, a private laugh that included the guys but only the guys, and they laughed with her. What could I do but laugh too and wonder why I was standing there with my knees showing out from under that uniform. Without looking I could see the blue-and-white triangle on my head, my hair shapeless in a net, my ankles thick in white oxfords. Nothing could have been less sheer than my stockings. There was this silence that came down right after I laughed. A silence it was her turn to fill up. With introductions, maybe, to her boyfriends or an invitation to sit down and have a Coke. Instead she lit a cigarette off the one she'd just finished and said, "We're on our way to the Coast. He's got an appointment with Hendrix." She gestured casually toward the boy next to her.

"Hendrix? Fantastic," I said. "Really fantastic. What's she doing now?"

Roberta coughed on her cigarette and the two guys rolled their eyes up at the ceiling.

"Hendrix. Jimi Hendrix, asshole. He's only the biggest—Oh, wow. Forget it."

I was dismissed without anyone saying good-bye, so I thought I would do it for her.

"How's your mother?" I asked. Her grin cracked her whole face. She swallowed. "Fine," she said. "How's yours?"

"Pretty as a picture," I said and turned away. The backs of my knees were damp. Howard Johnson's really was a dump in the sunlight.

James is as comfortable as a house slipper. He liked my cooking and I liked his big loud family. They have lived in Newburgh all of their lives and talk about it the way people do who have always known a home. His grandmother has a porch swing older than his father and when they talk about streets and avenues and buildings they call them names they no longer have. They still call the A&P Rico's because it stands on property, once a mom-and-pop store owned by Mr. Rico. And they call the new community college Town Hall because it once was. My mother-in-law puts up jelly and cucumbers and buys butter wrapped in cloth from a dairy. James and his father talk about fishing and baseball and I can see them all together on the Hudson in a raggedy skiff. Half the population of Newburgh is on welfare now, but to my husband's family it was still some upstate paradise of a time long past. A time of ice houses and vegetable wagons, coal furnaces and children weeding gardens. When our son was born my mother-in-law gave me the crib blanket that had been hers.

But the town they remembered had changed. Something quick was in the air. Magnificent old houses, so ruined they had become shelter for squatters and rent risks, were bought and renovated. Smart IBM people moved out of their suburbs back into the city and put shutters up and herb gardens in their backyards. A brochure came in the mail announcing the opening of a Food Emporium. Gourmet food, it said—and listed items the rich IBM crowd would want. It was located in a new mall at the edge of town and I drove out to shop there one day—just to see. It was late in June. After the tulips were gone and the Queen Elizabeth roses were open everywhere. I trailed my cart along the aisle tossing in smoked oysters and Robert's sauce and things I knew would sit in my cupboard for years. Only when I found some Klondike ice cream bars did I feel less guilty about spending James's fireman's salary so foolishly. My father-in-law ate them with the same gusto little Joseph did.

Waiting in the checkout line I heard a voice say, "Twyla!"

The classical music piped over the aisles had affected me and the woman leaning toward me was dressed to kill. Diamonds on her hand, a smart white summer dress. "I'm Mrs. Benson," I said.

"Ho. Ho. The Big Bozo," she sang.

For a split second I didn't know what she was talking about. She had a bunch of asparagus and two cartons of fancy water.

"Roberta!"

"Right."

"For heaven's sake. Roberta."

"You look great," she said.

"So do you. Where are you? Here? In Newburgh?"

"Yes. Over in Annandale."

I was opening my mouth to say more when the cashier called my attention to her empty counter.

"Meet you outside." Roberta pointed her finger and went into the express line.

I placed the groceries and kept myself from glancing around to check Roberta's progress. I remembered Howard

Johnson's and looking for a chance to speak only to be greeted with a stingy "wow." But she was waiting for me and her huge hair was sleek now, smooth around a small, nicely shaped head. Shoes, dress, everything lovely and summery and rich. I was dying to know what happened to her, how she got from Jimi Hendrix to Annandale, a neighborhood full of doctors and IBM executives. Easy, I thought. Everything is so easy for them. They think they own the world.

"How long," I asked her. "How long have you been here?"

"A year. I got married to a man who lives here. And you, you're married too, right? Benson, you said."

"Yeah. James Benson."

"And is he nice?"

"Oh, is he nice?"

"Well, is he?" Roberta's eyes were steady as though she really meant the question and wanted an answer.

"He's wonderful, Roberta. Wonderful."

"So you're happy."

"Very."

"That's good," she said and nodded her head. "I always hoped you'd be happy. Any kids? I know you have kids."

"One. A boy. How about you?"

"Four."

"Four?"

She laughed. "Stepkids. He's a widower."

"Oh."

"Got a minute? Let's have a coffee."

I thought about the Klondikes melting and the inconvenience of going all the way to my car and putting the bags in the trunk. Served me right for buying all that stuff I didn't need. Roberta was ahead of me.

"Put them in my car. It's right here."

And then I saw the dark blue limousine.

"You married a Chinaman?"

"No." She laughed. "He's the driver."

"Oh, my. If the Big Bozo could see you now."

We both giggled. Really giggled. Suddenly, in just a pulse beat, twenty years disappeared and all of it came rushing back. The big girls (whom we called gar girls—Roberta's misheard word for the evil stone faces described in a civics class) there dancing in the orchard, the ploppy mashed potatoes, the double weenies, the Spam with pineapple. We went into the coffee shop holding on to one another and I tried to think why we were glad to see each other this time and not before. Once, twelve years ago, we passed like strangers. A black girl and a white girl meeting in a Howard Johnson's on the road and having nothing to say. One in a blue-and-white triangle waitress hat, the other on her way to see Hendrix. Now we were behaving like sisters separated for much too long. Those four short months were nothing in time. Maybe it was the thing itself. Just being there, together. Two little girls who knew what nobody else in the world knew—how not to ask questions. How to believe what had to be believed. There was politeness in that reluctance and generosity as well. Is your mother sick too? No, she dances all night. Oh—and an understanding nod.

We sat in a booth by the window and fell into recollection like veterans.

"Did you ever learn to read?"

"Watch." She picked up the menu. "Special of the day. Cream of corn soup. Entrées. Two dots and a wriggly line. Quiche. Chef salad, scallops. . . ."

I was laughing and applauding when the waitress came up.

"Remember the Easter baskets?"

"And how we tried to *introduce* them?"

"Your mother with that cross like two telephone poles."

"And yours with those tight slacks."

We laughed so loudly heads turned and made the laughter hard to suppress.

"What happened to the Jimi Hendrix date?"

Roberta made a blow-out sound with her lips.

"When he died I thought about you."

"Oh, you heard about him finally?"

"Finally. Come on, I was a small-town country waitress."

"And I was a small-town country dropout. God, were we wild. I still don't know how I got out of there alive."

"But you did."

"I did. I really did. Now I'm Mrs. Kenneth Norton."

"Sounds like a mouthful."

"It is."

"Servants and all?"

Roberta held up two fingers.

"Ow! What does he do?"

"Computers and stuff. What do I know?"

"I don't remember a hell of a lot from those days, but Lord, St. Bonny's is as clear as daylight. Remember Maggie? The day she fell down and those gar girls laughed at her?"

Roberta looked up from her salad and stared at me. "Maggie didn't fall," she said.

"Yes, she did. You remember."

"No, Twyla. They knocked her down. Those girls pushed her down and tore her clothes. In the orchard."

"I don't—that's not what happened."

"Sure it is. In the orchard. Remember how scared we were?"

"Wait a minute. I don't remember any of that."

"And Bozo was fired."

"You're crazy. She was there when I left. You left before me."

"I went back. You weren't there when they fired Bozo."

"What?"

"Twice. Once for a year when I was about ten, another for two months when I was fourteen. That's when I ran away."

"You ran away from St. Bonny's?"

"I had to. What do you want? Me dancing in that orchard?"

"Are you sure about Maggie?"

"Of course I'm sure. You've blocked it, Twyla. It happened. Those girls had behavior problems, you know."

"Didn't they, though. But why can't I remember the Maggie thing?"

"Believe me. It happened. And we were there."

"Who did you room with when you went back?" I asked her as if I would know her. The Maggie thing was troubling me.

"Creeps. They tickled themselves in the night."

My ears were itching and I wanted to go home suddenly. This was all very well but she couldn't just comb her hair, wash her face, and pretend everything was hunky-dory. After the Howard Johnson's snub. And no apology. Nothing.

"Were you on dope or what that time at Howard Johnson's?" I tried to make my voice sound friendlier than I felt.

"Maybe, a little. I never did drugs much. Why?"

"I don't know, you acted sort of like you didn't want to know me then."

"Oh, Twyla, you know how it was in those days: black—white. You know how everything was."

But I didn't know. I thought it was just the opposite. Busloads of blacks and whites came into Howard Johnson's together. They roamed together then: students, musicians, lovers, protesters. You got to see everything at Howard Johnson's, and blacks were very friendly with whites in those days. But sitting there with nothing on my plate but two hard tomato wedges wondering about the melting Klondikes it seemed childish remembering the slight. We went to her car and, with the help of the driver, got my stuff into my station wagon.

"We'll keep in touch this time," she said.

"Sure," I said. "Sure. Give me a call."

"I will," she said, and then, just as I was sliding behind the wheel, she leaned into the window. "By the way. Your mother. Did she ever stop dancing?"

I shook my head. "No. Never."

Roberta nodded.

"And yours? Did she ever get well?"

She smiled a tiny sad smile. "No. She never did. Look, call me, okay?"

"Okay," I said, but I knew I wouldn't. Roberta had messed up my past somehow with that business about Maggie. I wouldn't forget a thing like that. Would I?

Strife came to us that fall. At least that's what the paper called it. Strife. Racial strife. The word made me think of a bird—a big shrieking bird out of 1,000,000,000 B.C. Flapping its wings and cawing. Its eye with no lid always bearing down on you. All day it screeched and at night it slept on the rooftops. It woke you in the morning, and from the *Today* show to the eleven o'clock news it kept you an awful company. I couldn't figure it out from one day to the next. I knew I was supposed to feel something strong, but I didn't know what, and James wasn't any help. Joseph was on the list of kids to be transferred from the junior high school to another one at some far-out-of-the-way place and I thought it was a good thing until I heard it was a bad thing. I mean I didn't know. All the schools seemed dumps to me, and the fact that one was nicer looking didn't hold much weight. But the papers were full of it and then the kids began to get jumpy. In August, mind you. Schools weren't even open yet. I thought Joseph might be frightened to go over there, but he didn't seem scared so I forgot about it, until I found myself driving along Hudson Street out there by the school they were trying to integrate and saw a line of women marching. And who do you suppose was in line, big as life, holding a sign in front of her bigger than her mother's cross? MOTHERS HAVE RIGHTS TOO! it said.

I drove on and then changed my mind. I circled the block, slowed down, and honked my horn.

Roberta looked over and when she saw me she waved. I didn't wave back, but I didn't move either. She handed her sign to another woman and came over to where I was parked.

"Hi."

"What are you doing?"

"Picketing. What's it look like?"

"What for?"

"What do you mean, 'What for?' They want to take my kids and send them out of the neighborhood. They don't want to go."

"So what if they go to another school? My boy's being bussed too, and I don't mind. Why should you?"

"It's not about us, Twyla. Me and you. It's about our kids."

"What's more *us* than that?"

"Well, it is a free country."

"Not yet, but it will be."

"What the hell does that mean? I'm not doing anything to you."

"You really think that?"

"I know it."

"I wonder what made me think you were different."

"I wonder what made me think you were different."

"Look at them," I said. "Just look. Who do they think they are? Swarming all over the place like they own it. And now they think they can decide where my child goes to school. Look at them, Roberta. They're Bozos."

Roberta turned around and looked at the women. Almost all of them were standing still now, waiting. Some were even edging toward us. Roberta looked at me out of some refrigerator behind her eyes. "No, they're not. They're just mothers."

"And what am I? Swiss cheese?"

"I used to curl your hair."

"I hated your hands in my hair."

The women were moving. Our faces looked mean to them of course and they looked as though they could not wait to throw themselves in front of a police car or, better yet, into my car and drag me away by my ankles. Now they surrounded my car and gently, gently began to rock it. I swayed back and forth like a sideways yo-yo. Automatically I reached for Roberta, like the old days in the orchard when they saw us watching them and we had to get out of there, and if one of us fell the other pulled her up and if one of us was caught the other stayed to kick and scratch, and neither would leave the other behind. My arm shot out of the car window but no receiving hand was there. Roberta was looking at me sway from side to side in the car and her face was still. My purse slid from the car seat down under the dashboard. The four policemen who had been drinking Tab in their car finally got the message and strolled over, forcing their way through the women. Quietly, firmly they spoke. "Okay, ladies. Back in line or off the streets."

Some of them went away willingly; others had to be urged away from the car doors and the hood. Roberta didn't move. She was looking steadily at me. I was fumbling to turn on the ignition, which wouldn't catch because the gearshift was still in drive. The seats of the car were a mess because the swaying had thrown my grocery coupons all over and my purse was sprawled on the floor.

"Maybe I am different now, Twyla. But you're not. You're the same little state kid who kicked a poor old black lady when she was down on the ground. You kicked a black lady and you have the nerve to call me a bigot."

The coupons were everywhere and the guts of my purse were bunched under the dashboard. What was she saying? Black? Maggie wasn't black.

"She wasn't black," I said.

"Like hell she wasn't, and you kicked her. We both did. You kicked a black lady who couldn't even scream."

"Liar!"

"You're the liar! Why don't you just go on home and leave us alone, huh?"

She turned away and I skidded away from the curb.

The next morning I went into the garage and cut the side out of the carton our portable TV had come in. It wasn't nearly big enough, but after a while I had a decent sign: red spray-painted letters on a white background— AND SO DO CHILDREN****. I meant just to go down to the school and tack it up somewhere so those cows on the picket line across the street could see it, but when I got there, some ten or so others had already assembled— protesting the cows across the street. Police permits and everything. I got in line and we strutted in time on our side while Roberta's group strutted on theirs. That first day we were all dignified, pretending the other side didn't exist. The second day there was name calling and finger gestures. But that was about all. People changed signs from time to time, but Roberta never did and neither did I. Actually my sign didn't make sense without Roberta's. "And so do children what?" one of the women on my side asked me. Have rights, I said, as though it was obvious.

Roberta didn't acknowledge my presence in any way, and I got to thinking maybe she didn't know I was there. I began to pace myself in the line, jostling people one minute and lagging behind the next, so Roberta and I could reach the end of our respective lines at the same time and there would be a moment in our turn when we would face each other. Still, I couldn't tell whether she saw me and knew my sign was for her. The next day I went early before we were scheduled to assemble. I waited until she got there before I exposed my new creation. As soon as she hoisted her MOTHERS HAVE RIGHTS TOO! I began to wave my new one, which said, HOW WOULD YOU KNOW? I know she saw that one, but I had gotten addicted now. My signs got crazier each day, and the women on my side decided that I was a kook. They couldn't make heads or tails out of my brilliant screaming posters.

I brought a painted sign in queenly red with huge black letters that said, IS YOUR MOTHER WELL? Roberta took her lunch break and didn't come back for the rest of the day or any day after. Two days later I stopped going too and couldn't have been missed because nobody understood my signs anyway.

It was a nasty six weeks. Classes were suspended and Joseph didn't go to anybody's school until October. The children—everybody's children—soon got bored with that extended vacation they thought was going to be so great. They looked at TV until their eyes flattened. I spent a couple of mornings tutoring my son, as the other mothers said we should. Twice I opened a text from last year that he had never turned in. Twice he yawned in my face. Other mothers organized living room sessions so the kids would keep up. None of the kids could concentrate, so they drifted back to *The Price Is Right* and *The Brady Bunch*. When the school finally opened there were fights once or twice and some sirens roared through the streets every once in a while. There were a lot of photographers from Albany. And just when ABC was about to send up a news crew, the kids settled down like nothing in the world had happened. Joseph hung my HOW WOULD YOU KNOW? sign in his bedroom. I don't know what became of AND SO DO CHILDREN****. I think my father-in-law cleaned some fish on it. He was always puttering around in our garage. Each of his five children lived in Newburgh, and he acted as though he had five extra homes.

I couldn't help looking for Roberta when Joseph graduated from high school, but I didn't see her. It didn't trouble me much what she had said to me in the car. I mean the kicking part. I know I didn't do that, I couldn't do that. But I was puzzled by her telling me Maggie was black. When I thought about it I actually couldn't be certain. She wasn't pitch-black, I knew, or I would have remembered that. What I remember was the kiddie hat and the semicircle legs. I tried to reassure myself about the race thing for a long time until it dawned on me that the truth was already there, and Roberta knew it. I didn't kick her; I didn't join in with the gar girls and kick that lady, but I sure did want to. We watched and never tried to help her and never called for help. Maggie was my dancing mother. Deaf, I thought, and dumb. Nobody inside. Nobody who would hear you if you cried in the night. Nobody who could tell you anything important that you could use. Rocking, dancing, swaying as she walked. And when the gar girls pushed her down and started rough-housing, I knew she wouldn't scream, couldn't—just like me—and I was glad about that.

We decided not to have a tree, because Christmas would be at my mother-in-law's house, so why have a tree at both places? Joseph was at SUNY New Paltz and we had to economize, we said. But at the last minute, I changed my mind. Nothing could be that bad. So I rushed around town looking for a tree, something small but wide. By the time I found a place, it was snowing and very late. I dawdled like it was the most important purchase in the world and the tree man was fed up with me. Finally I chose one and had it tied onto the trunk of the car. I drove away slowly because the sand trucks were not out yet and the streets could be murder at the beginning of a snowfall. Downtown the streets were wide and rather empty except for a cluster of people coming out of the Newburgh Hotel. The one hotel in town that wasn't built out of cardboard and Plexiglas. A party, probably. The men huddled in the snow were dressed in tails and the women had on furs. Shiny things glittered from underneath their coats. It made me tired to look at them. Tired, tired, tired. On the next corner was a small diner with loops and loops of paper bells in the window. I stopped the car and went in. Just for a cup of coffee and twenty minutes of peace before I went home and tried to finish everything before Christmas Eve.

"Twyla?"

There she was. In a silvery evening gown and dark fur coat. A man and another woman were with her, the man fumbling for change to put in the cigarette machine. The woman was humming and tapping on the counter with her fingernails. They all looked a little bit drunk.

"Well. It's you."

"How are you?"

I shrugged. "Pretty good. Frazzled. Christmas and all."

"Regular?" called the woman from the counter.

"Fine," Roberta called back and then, "Wait for me in the car."

She slipped into the booth beside me. "I have to tell you something, Twyla. I made up my mind if I ever saw you again, I'd tell you."

"I'd just as soon not hear anything, Roberta. It doesn't matter now, anyway."

"No," she said. "Not about that."

"Don't be long," said the woman. She carried two regulars to go and the man peeled his cigarette pack as they left.

"It's about St. Bonny's and Maggie."

"Oh, please."

"Listen to me. I really did think she was black. I didn't make that up. I really thought so. But now I can't be sure. I just remember her as old, so old. And because she couldn't talk—well, you know, I thought she was crazy. She'd been brought up in an institution like my mother was and like I thought I would be too. And you were right. We didn't kick her. It was the gar girls. Only them. But,

well, I wanted to. I really wanted them to hurt her. I said
we did it, too. You and me, but that's not true. And I don't
want you to carry that around. It was just that I wanted to
do it so bad that day—wanting to is doing it."

Her eyes were watery from the drinks she'd had, I
guess. I know it's that way with me. One glass of wine and
I start bawling over the littlest thing.

"We were kids, Roberta."

"Yeah. Yeah. I know, just kids."

"Eight."

"Eight."

"And lonely."

"Scared, too."

She wiped her cheeks with the heel of her hand and
smiled. "Well, that's all I wanted to say."

I nodded and couldn't think of any way to fill the
silence that went from the diner past the paper bells on out
into the snow. It was heavy now. I thought I'd better wait
for the sand trucks before starting home.

"Thanks, Roberta."

"Sure."

"Did I tell you? My mother, she never did stop
dancing."

"Yes. You told me. And mine, she never got well."
Roberta lifted her hands from the tabletop and covered her
face with her palms. When she took them away she really
was crying. "Oh, shit, Twyla. Shit, shit, shit. What the hell
happened to Maggie?"

Sandra Cisneros was born and grew up in Chicago, daughter of a Mexican father and a Mexican American mother. The two stories in this collection are from *The House on Mango Street*, a series of lyrical stories about coming of age as a Chicana, caught between the richness of her immigrant culture and the need to find her own place as an individual woman. She is also the author of *Woman Hollering Creek & Other Stories* and a volume of poetry *My Wicked, Wicked Ways*. She has worked as a teacher to high school dropouts, a poet-in-the-schools, a college recruiter, and a visiting writer to a number of universities around the country. She has received two NEA Fellowships for poetry and fiction. She lives in San Antonio, Texas.

Judith Ortiz Cofer was born in Puerto Rico, and moved to Paterson, New Jersey, traveling back and forth between the island and Paterson during her childhood. *In Silent Dancing: A Partial Remembrance of a Puerto Rican Childhood*, she blends autobiography and poetry. She is associate professor of English and creative writing at the University of Georgia. "Bad Influence" is from her collection *An Island Like You: Stories of the Barrio*, which was chosen as a Best Book for Young Adults by the American Library Association and a Booklist Editors' Choice.

Francisco Jiménez was born in Mexico and came to California as a child with his family to work in the fields as migrant workers. He is now a U.S. citizen who is a university professor, an anthologist of short stories in Spanish and English, and the author of many short stories. "The Circuit" received the 22nd Arizona Quarterly Annual Award for Best Short Story. The University of New Mexico Press is publishing Jiménez's collection of twelve semi-autobiographical short stories, *The Circuit: Stories from the Life of a Migrant Child* in 1997.

Edward P. Jones' "The First Day" is from *Lost in the City*, a collection of short stories about African American life in Washington, D.C., nominated for a 1992 National Book Award. Jones attended the College of the Holy Cross at the University of Virginia. He lives in Arlington, Virginia.

Norma Fox Mazer grew up in Glen Falls, New York. She has been writing all her life and is the author of many acclaimed young adult books, including *After the Rain* (a Newbery Honor book) and *The Solid Gold Kid* (co-authored with her husband, novelist Harry Mazer). "Zelzah" is from a collection of stories *Dear Bill, Remember Me?* (a *New York Times* Outstanding Book of the Year and an ALA Best Book for Young Adults).

Toni Morrison won the Nobel Prize for Literature in 1993. She has been a teacher, an editor, and is currently Professor in the Council of the Humanities at Princeton. She is the co-chair of the Schomburg Commission for the Preservation of Black Culture. She has a B.A. in English from Howard University and a Master of Arts from Cornell. Her earliest acclaimed novels are *The Bluest Eye, Sula,* and *Tar Baby;* her most recent is *Jazz.* She won the Pulitzer Prize for Fiction in 1988 for *Beloved.* Born in Lorain, Ohio, Morrison says, "I am from the Midwest, so I have special affection for it. My beginnings are always there . . ."

Charles Mungoshi is a well-known Zimbabwean writer, who received international PEN awards for his writing in 1976 and 1981. "The Setting Sun and the Rolling World" is the title story from his prize-winning collection of 17 stories first published in the United States in 1989. His children's book, *One Day, Long Ago,* which includes stories from his Shona childhood, won the African prize, the Noma Award, in 1992.

Tim O'Brien grew up in Minnesota, attended Macalester College and Harvard University, and served as a foot soldier in Vietnam. "On the Rainy River" is from *The Things They Carried,* about a twenty-three-year-old foot soldier and an older writer remembering his war experience. He is the author of *Going after Cacciato.* His latest acclaimed novel is *In the Lake of the Woods.*

David St. John is the author of five collections of poetry, including *Study for the World's Body,* HarperCollins, 1994, which was nominated for the National Book Award in Poetry. He is the Asian and European Editor of *The Antioch Review* (where he served as Poetry Editor for fifteen years) and professor of English at The University of Southern California.

Annette Sanford's first story, "A Child's Game," won a first-place award from the Catholic Press Association. Her fiction has appeared in many publications, including *Prairie Schooner, Ohio Review,* and *Redbook.* She was awarded a Creative Writing Fellowship Grant from the National Endowment for the Arts. "Trip in a Summer Dress" was chosen for *Best American Short Stories of 1979,* edited by Joyce Carol Oates. Sanford is a former teacher who lives in Ganado, Texas.

Vickie Sears is a Cherokee writer and teacher whose poetry and short stories have appeared in several journals and story collections, including *Spider Woman's Granddaughters: Traditional Tales and Contemporary Writing by Native American Women.* "Dancer" appears in *Talking Leaves: Contemporary Native American Short Stories.* She has also published *Simple Songs: Stories by Vickie Sears.*

Allan Sherman, born in Chicago, was a writer, singer, comedian, and television producer. He won two Gold Albums in 1962 for "My Son, the Folk Singer" and "My Son, the Celebrity." He won a Grammy Award in 1963 for the best comic performance for his song, "Hello Muddah, Hello Fadduh," a young boy's letter home from summer camp. He wrote for comedians Jackie Gleason, Victor Borge, and Phil Silvers. The story in this anthology is from *A Gift of Laughter: The Autobiography of Allan Sherman.*

Gary Soto was born in Fresno, California, and grew up in and around the fields of the San Joaquin Valley, the subject of his autobiographical collections *Small Faces, Living Up the Street,* and *A Summer Life.* He has written poetry and fiction for adults. His work for young adults includes the short story collection, *Baseball in April,* and *Pacific Crossing.* He has produced three short films, including "The Pool Party," which was awarded the Andrew Carnegie Medal for Excellence in Children's Video.

Amy Tan was born and raised in Oakland, California. She received a B.A. and an M.A. from San Jose State University. "The Rules of the Game" is from *The Joy Luck Club,* which tells the stories of four Chinese American women and their daughters living in contemporary San Francisco. It was on the *New York Times* Bestseller List for over nine months and was translated into seventeen languages, including Chinese. She wrote the script for the movie version. She has written two other novels, *The Kitchen God's Wife* and *The Hundred Secret Senses.* Amy Tan lives in San Francisco.

Tim Wynne-Jones is a children's book editor who lives in Perth, Ontario, in Canada. He is the author of several books for young people as well as adult fiction, the book and libretto for an opera, and a children's musical. He also writes music for his rock band, The Suspects. "Dawn" is from his collection of stories, *The Book of Changes,* which features some of the same characters that appeared in his award-winning *Some of the Kinder Planets.* His latest novel is *The Maestro.*

Acknowledgments

Thanks are due to the following for permission to reprint the copyrighted materials listed below:

Robert Bly. Two lines from "The Way In" (used as an epigraph) from *Selected Poems of Rainer Maria Rilke*, edited and translated by Robert Bly. Reprinted by permission of HarperCollins Publishers.

Sandra Cisneros. "A House of My Own" and "Beautiful & Cruel" are from *The House on Mango Street*. Copyright ©1984 by Sandra Cisneros. Published by Vintage Books, a division of Random House, Inc., New York and in hardcover by Alfred A. Knopf in 1994. Reprinted by permission of Susan Bergholz Literary Services, New York. All rights reserved.

Judith Ortiz Cofer. "Bad Influence" from *An Island Like You* by Judith Ortiz Cofer. ©1995 by Judith Ortiz Cofer. Reprinted by permission of Orchard Books, New York.

Francisco Jiménez. "The Circuit" © 1973 by Francisco Jiménez. Reprinted by permission of Francisco Jiménez. All rights reserved.

Edward P. Jones. Text of "First Day," from *Lost in the City* by Edward P. Jones. Text copyright © 1992 by Edward P. Jones. Reprinted by permission of William Morrow & Co., Inc.

Norma Fox Mazer. "Zelzah: A Tale From Long Ago" from *Dear Bill, Remember Me? and Other Stories* by Norma Fox Mazer. Copyright © 1976 by Norma Fox Mazer. Used by permission of Dell Books, a division of Bantam Doubleday Dell Publishing Group, Inc.

Toni Morrison. "Recitatif" by Toni Morrison is reprinted by permission of International Creative Management, Inc. Copyright © 1983 by Toni Morrison.

Charles Mungoshi. "The Setting Sun and the Rolling World" from *The Setting Sun and the Rolling World* by Charles Mungoshi. Copyright © 1972, 1980 by Charles Mungoshi. Reprinted by permission of Beacon Press, Boston.

Tim O'Brien. "On the Rainy River" from *The Things They Carried*. Copyright © 1990 by Tim O'Brien. Reprinted by permission of Houghton Mifflin Co./Seymour Lawrence. All rights reserved.

Annette Sanford. "Trip in a Summer Dress" by Annette Sanford. Copyright © 1989 by Annette Sanford. Reproduced by permission of the author. All rights reserved.

Vickie Sears. "Dancer" by Vickie Sears from *Simple Songs*, Firebrand Books, Ithaca, New York. Copyright © 1990 by Vickie Sears.

Allan Sherman. Reprinted with the permission of Scribner, a Division of Simon & Schuster from *A Gift of Laughter* by Allan Sherman. Copyright © 1965 by Allan Sherman.

Gary Soto. "Saturday at the Canal" from *Home Course in Religion* by Gary Solo © 1991, published by Chronicle Books, San Francisco.

David St. John. "Little Saigon" © by David St. John. Reprinted by permission of David St. John. All rights reserved.

Amy Tan. Reprinted by permission of G. P. Putnam's Sons from "Rules of the Game" from *The Joy Luck Club* by Amy Tan. Copyright © 1989 by Amy Tan.

Tim Wynne-Jones. "Dawn" from *The Book of Changes* by Tim Wynne-Jones. Copyright © 1994 by Tim Wynne-Jones. Reprinted by permission of Orchard Books, New York, and by permission of Groundwood Books/Douglas & McIntyre.